PARIS LOVE SUICIDE

Hillary Raphael

Future Fiction London

futurefictionlondon.com

ISBN 978-0-9827928-8-9

To all those who lost their lives to COVID-19

Editor's Note

A posthumous publication is always a complexity. Faced with the impossibility of rewrites or even consent for edits, the editor must tread lightly. It is with this in mind that I ask the reader to find in this manuscript inter-est of a sociological, criminological, linguistic, even epidemiological nature. Don't expect lit-erary pleasures you'll only be disappointed not to have found. As a time capsule of Paris at the outbreak of 2020's pandemic crisis, the notebook of the young French-Canadian woman, Huguette L___ fits the bill.

With the exception of the chronicler her-self, all names have been changed. In the same interest of anonymity, whole sections of the original manuscript have been cut. These episodes identified individuals not previously identified by investigative journalists in *Paris Match* and other outlets. A short word on the text: A non-native English speaker and an untrained writer, our narrator's voice is refreshing for its rawness and authenticity. Where a word is rendered in French, the italics are mine. She abused the semicolon. She loved adverbs, to put it mildly, and was often repetitive, but the reader who can move past these marks of the amateur will enjoy manifold rewards.

We'll never hear the voices of the vast majority of those whose lives were taken by COVID-19. That Huguette L___ became embroiled in a tragedy in which the public has taken a prurient interest should only be seen as a fortunate conduit to our encounter with the notes she took during the distressing period that will resonate in contemporary history for time to come. The author of this notebook died the lonely death of all those plastic hooded in the Intensive Care Unit, with a ventilator as her last companion. It is with gratitude to her that these pages are presented. Guilty or not in the eyes of the law, hers was one innocent soul among many to be stilled by the virus.

Thanks are due as well to The Fund For Arts and Letters of Québec, without whose support this publication could not exist.

- ADELAIDE COMBAZ-MURPHY, Paris

I can remember the date of the first time I set eyes on him very perfectly because it was the first day they shut down the Louvre because of Coronavirus. I recall thinking, right before he walked in, that it must have been the first time in a while that the Mona Lisa found herself free of idiots taking their own picture in front of her. The Mona Lisa has entered my mind several times while I'm being questioned by the police, with that poor bored guy from the Canadian Consular Wing always at my elbow. I think he is considered my lawyer. He seems sometimes frustrated by my responses, or by my manner. Sometimes, when a question makes no sense to me, I default to a Mona Lisa smirk, which annoys everyone, but makes me feel a little better. I've never been conventionally attractive; neither is she, but like her, I emanate a certain *je ne sais quoi* that fascinates certain people, but only males.

It's funny: as a Canadian citizen, I have the right to be questioned in English. I decided to take them up on it, never mind that it's my second language. It was my best subject in primary school and I've always liked speaking it. Even if I sound a bit off, I like the way it helps me clarify my thoughts. Languages do that. Each one has a different effect on the mind, like a drug. Japanese makes me dreamy. English is like a cold shower, nice and healthy. For me, French is … complicated. When I first got here, my Québécois accent was so strong, people couldn't understand me. Or maybe they just pretended that. You never know. People are so cruel. Plenty mocked my accent, too. Over time, I filed down its edges. Now my accent is smoother, more generic. Perhaps if I go back to Montréal some time, they'd make fun of me there. But I don't think so. They're really so much nicer than Parisians. If our cute, harmless separatists had had their way, I'd have gotten a Francophone lawyer from a Québec embassy, but for better or worse, that never happened, so I am still, tangentially, a subject of the Queen, and setting aside all the Brexit folly, I can't say I mind that. My thoughts are interrupted by a new person entering the room, a woman in a skirt and pumps this time, asking if I'd like a coffee. "Earl Grey tea, please," I say with a straight face, "in a white porcelain pot." Nervous laughter, unsure if I'm kidding or bonkers. I go back to the enigmatic smirk. At least I didn't specify Limoges china, which is what I brew it in, in my little flat. I miss my little flat and hope to go home to it soon.

* * *

On the morning of March first 2020, I woke up naturally, without an alarm because it was Sunday and I do not work on Sundays. The shop, however, is open on Sundays, but I do not have a shift then. Usually the owner Shizuka, after whom Boutique Shizuka is named-- I believe the English word is "eponymous"-- works by herself that day. I woke up when I felt like it, or when the light raindrops on the shutters became disruptive enough. I love my shutters. They're painted black and they're the only classic detail my flat has got. We've no spiral staircase or herring-bone parquet floor or bidet, but we have these lovely shutters, just perfect for this mild climate. Compared to Montréal, most of the world has a mild climate, but I find Paris, with its spittling mists and fickle cloud cover, especially so. Every morning, the small space fills up with the perfume of bergamot as I brew the day's first tea in my flawless white Limoges pot, which has sixteen thin black lines around its middle like strokes of a fine point pen, bookended by two thin gold rings. The lid has the same two gilt stripes, but only ten concentric black rings. My cup doesn't match, but no matter. I adore blue and white transferware just as much. It would probably be better if I were the kind of person who had plain yogurt with hemp hearts for breakfast, or maybe green juice, or even just Japanese water therapy, but I always have starch and sugar with my tea. Sometimes I have the time and the will to dash out for fresh croissants, bring them back in a nice, crinkly sack. Sometimes it's a chunk of yesterday's baguette, freshened up with jam or choco-hazelnut stuff. That particular morning, I put on my lucky bright yellow rain jacket that I'd found on a bench in the Luxembourg Garden-- can you imagine just forgetting about an Armour Lux? Madness-- and went out, hood drawn up and tied, to buy a couple of *chocolatines*. It was so cozy getting home with them, hanging the wet slicker on the rack by the door, finding the kettle still warm, near boiling, brewing my Earl Grey, and having my breakfast next to the window. Breakfast is a highlight. Another highlight is red lipstick. It was Helena Rubinstein who said there are no ugly women, only lazy ones. I also keep my nails red and never chipped. My genes are not my fault, but my choices are. I have made good choices. I have exactly one of every thing needed to be chic. I have one pair of black calfskin ballet flats for work. I have one silk Hermès scarf that I bought at a *friperie* (I never say "friperie" in English. "Thrift shop" sounds so threadbare). I confess that I stole my good strand of Akoya pearls from a store customer who took them off in the fitting room to try something on, then left them behind. In fact, I was just keeping them for her until... she actually did come back for them, and feeling the rose gold clasp in my pocket, I spontaneously lied and said I'd never seen them. They've become the anchor of my chic.

Sadly though, chic is only conformity to a strict set of guidelines that tells others we're cognizant enough and prosperous enough to adhere to them. It's not much different from a policeman's uniform. That morning, as I dusted the last of the crumbs off the tabletop into my open palm, and overturned my palm into the trash, I decided to stop by the shop anyway to pick up a paycheck owed me. Shizuka, who has a somewhat flighty demeanour, had had some technical problems with the computer or the printer or both, in the cramped, surprisingly untidy back office and had been unable to pay me on payday. She'd subsequently left me a message saying she'd managed to print my check and I could come pick it up on my day off if I didn't want to wait until Tuesday. Why not?, I thought, what else have I got to do?

When I got there around mid-day, I carefully placed my folded-up umbrella in the rack so as not to scatter any raindrops on the floor. Shizuka was fawning all over a customer, the only one in the store, a man in a black nylon trench coat with a reflective tab on the weather flap. His back was to me. I nodded at Shizuka in her peripheral vision, just tersely enough to show that I had no intention of interrupting, would just pop into the office. She didn't register my presence as she expounded, in a bright Japanese, on the different fibre contents of the various split-toe socks on offer. I slipped behind the mirrored door, grabbed my envelope, and stuffed it into the navy blue Longchamp crossbody bag I wear any time I go to work. As I re-emerged onto the floor, trying to be as invisible as possible, Shizuka was making a lot of satisfied, efficient noise individually wrapping a dozen pairs of socks in purple tissue paper. I guess the customer had found what he'd wanted. I intended to take my umbrella and leave with another unacknowledged nod, but as I crossed the floor with my chin tucked into my chest, she surprised me by saying to him, "Well, let's ask her," then switching to French to say in an imperious tone, "Huguette, join us for a moment?" Shizuka speaks French with an accent so thick, it pains me to imagine how anyone who's not familiar with Japanese can ever understand her. However, I would never try to reproduce it in mimicry or italics or any-thing like that. I couldn't imagine either what on earth I could add to her sock sale transac-tion, but I am generally not particularly imagi-native. I sidled over to the cash, which is just a mounted tablet next to a crystal jar of mints and a stack of business cards embossed in gold. Then, something happened to me on a cellular level, a clicking shift, a shifting click of solidifying fluids when I looked into her cus-tomer's face. The shapes and planes of it res-onated with unmet desires, answers to questions I'd once asked in a dream, then forgotten. His accent was as Japanese as hers, just less abusive to French. "Where do you get your hair coloured?" After a moment's blank stare, I said that it's natural. I didn't say that my burning red hair is my only physical attribute ever to be considered strikingly beautiful by anyone, that it is prettier than my beautiful sister's dark brown, that the only other time it's been seen in my family was on my father's great-aunt Marie-Josée, but that it's a relatively prevalent gene in the French-Canadian population, and that everyone thinks I dye it because of the missing naturalness markers of light eyes and freckles. I was still staring and thinking when I was dismissed, later finding myself under my umbrella, walking towards ballet class.

To attend a ballet class once a week is to admit defeat. It means that over the course of god knows how many years, you'd given up on the idea of going pro, then even on the idea of performing in amateur recitals (which would have dropped you down to maybe three times a week), and finally even given up on ballet as a means of maintaining fitness. My own once-a-week routine is hard to fathom. It keeps me just within grazing grasp of tender muscle soreness and gauzy pink hosiery. I've been at it since I was four and have always comforted my classmates by being fat. As long as I'm next to you in the mirror, you're slender. I've been in the same class since moving here; its damp air and splintered barre reassure me. There's a Nespresso pod vending machine in the corridor and usually outdated magazines left behind by mothers waiting out the earlier classes. I can remember very perfectly the cover of the *Paris Match* that was tossed on a metal folding chair that day because the sight of his face had done something to my eyes that made them into efficient cameras. It was a photo of the arrest of that beautiful girl who leaked Benjamin Girveaux's masturbatory videos to the press, causing him to drop his mayoral bid and embarrassing his pregnant wife. *Plié, plié, plié*. When I was a little girl, I didn't know that all the world practices ballet in French. I used to think that the Anglophones said it all in English, like "Bent, thrown, hit."

Bent, thrown, hit. I have exactly one friend in my ballet class, but when I was little, my mother always told me that one is all you need. Therefore, I'm golden. Yvonne is in this class thanks to a hip replacement. When she was my age and younger, she danced seriously, at times professionally, training six hours a day. She also was married before I knew her. You could say that her misfortunes just levelled the playing field enough that she was primed to befriend me the day I took my first uncertain step over the threshold. We have the pleasant habit of going to her house after class for croissants and hot chocolate. She prepares it especially viscous. Her careful, deliberate first bite, with its delightful recoil from the crunch always tells me it's her first of the day, while it's always at least my third. It's really good to have friends different from oneself. It expands one's horizons. That day--

The girl policeman, the one in a black pantsuit, (I can't see her shoes), robin's egg blue button-down shirt, pearl studs and rose gold Fitbit, interrupts to ask, somewhat obtusely, "Which day are we talking about?"

I clarify in English, "The day I first met him, saw him," which the interpreter relays back in French. Everyone at the table knows this interpreter is unnecessary, but I like having her here. She puts distance between me and the awfulness.

That day, Yvonne put out a delicious mango-peach *confiture*, so our hands and mouths were busy for a few silent minutes. I could feel the sugar racing into my blood-stream, hurrying to make me feel good. The rain had stopped. Bright light suffused the kitchen. It felt so nice to enjoy companionship on an early Spring day off. Elsewhere in the city, others were working their butts off in the manic daze of Fashion Week. Others were fainting from hunger, pricking their thumbs on pins, being upbraided by a superior, being splashed with puddle mud by a taxi, but not us. *En plus*, we had a pretty church and healthy sycamores to look at. A married man had bought her this apartment as a present a long time ago-- I won't give the exact location because her neighbors never did anything wrong, just well-heeled, courteous people with little dogs. Anyway, it was a little above her current circumstances. Her cup, white with pink carnations, clattered a little as she set it down into its saucer mate, whose scalloped edges I always loved. The light caught on that gold pearlescent nail polish she wore. It twinkled like she'd brought a sample of the river home with her. Wanting to live up to the occasion, I offered, "I met a man of great distinction today." My word choice might have been pandering, but the sentiment was accurate. I couldn't stop re-feeling the impact of that face on my mind. His eyes were teaching me something about reality, but the lesson was still incomplete. Yvonne asked me a battery of questions about him that I couldn't answer, so we agreed that I should try to bump into him again.

About once a week, I have a video chat with my sister. I would have preferred plain audio, but her vanity demands that she showcase herself whenever possible. I can't blame her. All her life, she's been told that her beauty is important, so I guess it has become that. I do blame her, though, for regurgitating every instance of someone telling her we don't look like sisters. Or even members of the same family, as she tells it. She rang me punctually that night, right after I'd wrapped my shampooed hair in a terry turban and just as I was

tucking into a microwaved quiche lorraine. I
poured myself a glass of Pinot Noir as she rattled off her week's accomplishments. I'd need
a second glass before it was my turn to talk;
she'd had so many unexpected *coups*. I
chewed and gulped noisily, but from what I
could gather: she'd sold out all the slots at a
yoga retreat she was running in a mountain
lake-side forest; her child made the tiny tot
hockey team at the community center most
convenient to them; her husband received a
research and development tax holiday from the
province for his startup; maybe a few other
things, was she pregnant or getting a Sanskrit
tattoo? Or an electric car? It was my turn.
Well, almost. First, she wanted to know if I'd
heard about Intermittent Fasting. One of her
students had had a lot of "success" with it.
When it was my real turn, I was loathe to report
just that I'd sold several antique kimonos, a
bunch of silver necklaces, and coin purses

made out of obis, and had taken my weekly dance class. I also had made a risotto, but she wouldn't approve. Keeping in the spirit of the *coups*, I announced proudly, "A very handsome customer invited me out."

"Huguette, shouldn't you not fraternize with customers?"

"Why ever not?" I was outraged for this dampening of my artificial fun.

"Huguette. It's unprofessional, not to say unethical."

"What are you talking about, Coco? I'm not a college professor. Or a therapist. Why would one avoid a boutique shopper?"

She sighed. "Just common decency. Anyway, don't you sell ladies' clothes?"

"Now we stock men's stuff too. Don't you wanna know what he looks like?"

"Sure." Coralie's bored voice is so practiced and so transparently cultivated.

"Almond eyes of a jet-like opacity. Deli-cate, hairless nostrils. Poreless skin--"

"Wait."

"I wasn't finished."

"Huguette, why are all your descriptors about absence? No hairs, no pores. It's like you resent men for existing."

"Wrong. I was about to say, when you interrupted me, wide, geometric mouth, broadly spaced stubble--"

"Just tell me if he's bald, like you-know-who."

"God, Coco, you're really superficial. Well, I don't know. He was wearing a Paris Saint-Germain cap."

"Ok, finally you're saying something good. He sounds more normal than you're ac-customed to."

"I'll ignore that. In any case, he invited me to a cocktail, so I'm going to get a *brushing*."

I love getting a *brushing*. The scent of not-my-home-shampoo and the feel of some-one else's fingers kneading my scalp. And of course they always say my hair is beautiful, a thick mane of cascading lava, like an erupting volcano. But I seldom have the cash for one.

Tuesday morning, I woke up early to blow out my own hair before work. I wanted to be my best self because I had big plans. I opened the shop with my own set of keys, and went through all the motions that were so sec-ond nature as to spring from muscle memory, while my mind frolicked elsewhere. I fed the goldfish in their bulbous glass bowl. Changed the water in the vase of silk flowers to make them look real. Re-straightened all the racks and stacks. Replenished any of the Indian rings that had been sold, filling in any empty spaces in the black velvet display case. Dusted the countertop and the wall mounted leather schoolchild satchels. Lit a sandalwood candle. Normally, after that, I stared vacantly until the day's first customer came in, rousing me like a voice-activated A.I. This time, I rubbed my hands together like a child actor expressing enthused satisfaction. I intended to will my half-truths into full truths. I rifled around until I found the sales slip I was looking for. The forensics were easy-- no one else had bought a bunch of men's *tabi*. Split-toe socks are a less commonly desired item in Paris in general, so we didn't see many such sales slips ever. Found it. The paper stared back at me wide eyed, like a winning lottery ticket, stunned at itself. This flimsy, white Rosetta Stone of de-sire, no, wrong metaphor, it answered rather than translated, my questions, more like a Holy Ark. I quickly took a photo of it and put it away, so if Shizuka staged one of her pernicious sur-prises, the worst she'd see was an employee looking at her phone, hardly atypical.

His name: Masahisa Mori

Address: I'd need to google map it later on. I'm not a mail carrier or taxi driver who can glance at an address and toss out, "Oh, that's in the eleventh," am I?

Phone number: x xx xx xx xx, a local number

E-mail: bonjour@masacoupe.fr

That was a lot of info right there. I even had his approximate shoe size, pretty *petit* for a man, and his bank. I wondered what kind of tea he drank. Was he the one-tea type of person, who drinks the same thing all the time? I could see that. There's a certain steadfast elegance to it. Or was he a classic seasonal brewer, like barley and stems in the summer, leaves in the winter kind of guy? I secretly hoped he was like me, and even thought he was, but I didn't want to get ahead of myself. I choose my tea according to my mood, looking through my own window at the interior weather before deciding. I take a jasmine green when erotic sensations threaten to overwhelm me, and that's exactly what I made first thing getting home that evening.

* * *

"Let's get to the evening of Monday, March nine." Just as she says this, the detective's Fitbit buzzes, maybe reminding her to stretch her legs, and she taps it without looking. There's a knock at the door. "*Entrez*," she says, also without looking. A uniformed cop, young but with an old geezer moustache, or maybe this is a style statement, sets a round tray, the standard one from all cafés, down on the table between us. We each get a tiny cardboard cup of coffee, black. My man from the embassy asks for cream. I request Canderel, the French Splenda. The cop goes out for them immediately, like a waiter. The lighting in here is horrible. When I look down at my own hand, it's sallow, almost jaundiced. I'd love to take a walk through the park, if it weren't for this damn cane. And of course, this interview. The crisp Anglo voice saying, "She's already taken you through the night of the ninth four times," followed by the interpreter's peeved-sounding version. I'm not up to that night yet, though. I'm still getting through the days leading up to it. They'll have to be patient and bring in sandwiches.

I deliberately didn't ask Shizuka about the encounter with the *tabi* customer, no matter how tempting it was. Another woman in my shoes would surely have broken down and asked something like, "Why did that customer want to know about my hair?" just to open a dialogue about him, but I resisted. I have found that silence is best in most situations.

When I'm agitated, a standard sencha, slightly over brewed, clears my head. I forced myself, the second I got home, to watch it steep for three minutes before I would be allowed to look up masacoupe.fr. The timer beeped. I poured the grassy liquid into a chipped Wood & Sons English Scenery cup, and settled in front of my rickety old laptop as at a burning hearth. Tap tap tap tap tap ... tap tap tap tap tap tap ... tap. Twelve times. I've had cause, since then, to wonder if I wouldn't have been better off never typing that url at all, never following the Contact link to a map, never getting sucked into all the photos of gorgeous girls on his pages. Shouldn't I have minded my own business, as my mother used to admonish me by the dozens of repetitions? But you have to remember that it was he who started with me. Why'd he have to know about my hair anyway, huh?

I learned that he had to know because he was a successful, even legendary hairdresser. Masa Coupe was apparently an in-demand hair salon with, if I understood the online booking system, a months-long wait for a first appointment. The price list read like a Michelin-starred menu, an idea at least partially fueled by such mouth-watering treatments as

the Milk & Honey Deep Conditioning and the
Black Licorice Hair Gloss. It looked like he'd
been known to coif Carla Bruni. I was glad she
was out of the Elysée, but the sight of her still
rankled. She always had a touch of my sister
Coralie about her, hard to say exactly how, just
a certain entitled, healthily malnourished
brunette air. The time vanished, as it does,
and it was past my habitual bedtime before I'd
exhausted Masa's feed. I skipped dinner to fall
directly into my dreams. Dream is my favorite
word in Japanese: *yūme*. When you say it,
your mouth is left open in stupefaction. With
my native *rêve*, the mouth ends up shut, as
though you'd been abruptly awoken and the
dream ended. I was an exceptional language
student. My family and friends had all thought I
was nuts to major in Japanese, but I was so
good at it, such a rare feeling. I could reproduce the characters on command, like a friendly ghost was in my hand, guiding stoke after
well-placed stroke. I had thought that by now

I'd be a translator of poetry, something deep and beautiful, the person who wrote the supertitles for the Noh theatre when it tours abroad. It sometimes startles me that I work in a boutique, that without the sales commissions, my salary would barely sustain me, but *c'est la vie.* The good news is I got away from my hometown and I invented my own life, whatever it is. How many people really end up in the *métier* they'd imagined? Did Masahisa want to do hair as a little boy?

On my way to work that Wednesday, I stopped in at a pharmacy for more hand sanitizer, but it was sold out. That chilled me to the bone. I hadn't thought I'd wanted masks or gloves, but upon seeing the sign that apologized for their lack of availability, I hungered for them with a brisk anxiety. Shizuka was waiting for me at the shop with an ashen face to match her grey *ombré* nails. The nails of her ring fingers twinkled, *kira kira*, with micro-rhinestones.

"You weren't answering your phone," she accused.

"Oh sorry, sometimes I forget to turn the volume back on in the morning. Hate to be woken by telemarketers at night." Telemarketers At Night sounded like a cover band. My boss always lets the right side of her left-parted long hair fall forward to obscure her face when she's experiencing negative emotions. She keeps it so thoroughly dyed black that it obliterates light rather than reflects it. "I was trying to let you know, Huguette, that we'll be closed until further notice. We can't have people stepping in here, coughing all over the merchandise and killing us in the process, can we?"

"No, of course not, but what about my salary?"

"I can afford to pay you for half-time. Sorry."

Was that even legal? I bookmarked the question for later, choosing instead to ask, "Do you have any supplies? Masks and stuff?" Everyone has one type of situation they're perfect in. This was Shizuka's. She always arrives well-stocked to the picnic of life-- when it starts raining, she's the one to move the blanket under a giant umbrella and to pass out disposable ponchos to the guests. Parting her pursed, peach glossed lips to form the bleached rectangle that is her smile, she wordlessly handed me a glossy store gift bag, looking for all the world like a catwalk swag bag, but stuffed with rows of anti-viral supplies. I thanked her profusely. She bid me please persevere and let me show myself out.

Unaccustomed to freedom in the middle of a weekday, I stood on the pavement around the corner, gripping the bag and panning three-hundred-sixty degrees around myself, not sure how to proceed. Then with the inscrutable clarity of an early morning dream, I tapped a destination into my maps app, settled a blue surgical mask over my face, snapped on a pair of matching rubber gloves, pulled up the hood of my black wool agnès b. anorak, and methodically followed the trail of dots all the way to Masa Coupe. It was a long walk, through at least three different weather conditions and across the Seine. It's funny that here they call the river *"rivière"* when it's actually a *fleuve*, like my St. Laurent, which flows into the ocean. No matter, they're very good at creating their own reality here. I walked by the place once, but at too fast a clip to get a good look inside-- just a blur of clean white shirts and a potted orchid. I turned around and walked by more slowly, slow enough to make out faces of employees, but none wore the mask of intrigue and desire I'd glimpsed before. My heart sank. I found a vacant bench in a vest pocket park across the street and sat down to regroup. My thoughts were scattering like confetti, so I pulled a pencil and a tiny orange Clairefontaine notebook out

of my purse. I wrote down all the possibilities.
He could not be there (day off or out on a shoot
or backstage at a show or calling on a client) or
he could be there (at a station away from the
window, or in a back office or out on coffee
break). The only way to know was to wait. I
had a good view of the door, though none of
the interior. The light's reflection on the windows made them, for the time being, opaque.
That meant I'd need to fix a steady gaze on the

doorway. I wouldn't want to look away just as
he was coming in or out and then, unable to
see inside, be none the wiser to his presence.
The bathroom could become a problem, so I
resolved not to eat or drink. That would surely
be healthy anyway. The mind does funny
things when the body is still. As the clouds
shuffled themselves above and the puddles below rippled and stilled, my thoughts flew like
petals in a storm: For all the compliments I got
on my hair everyday of my life, I had next to no
experience with salons. I cut mine myself us-

ing a nail scissor and two mirrors over the bathroom sink. The women who came and went through the door, that door I'd glued my eyes to like goggly eyes on a kindergarten craft card, these women looked so well-funded, like people who couldn't recall their last bad day, bad hair day or otherwise. I remembered other crafts I made when I was little, notably a picture frame made of markered-up popsicle sticks to go around my kindergarten graduation photo. They had never been licked clean of fudgsicle though. Mrs. Tremblay had explained that that would have been unsanitary because of the bacteria in saliva and it would not have been ecologically sound to wash that many, so she had purchased ones made of recycled wood at a craft shop. Each of our parents would be billed a toonie. In retrospect, none of that made sense. My thirst must have been getting to me because I became firmly convinced that Masahisa was a drinker of *genmaicha*, a masculine tea thanks to its roasted brown rice kernels, but not too macho thanks to the uplifting raw green in the mix. Macho made me think of *macha*-- macho/ macha, macha/ macho-- and the spidery whisks they used to froth it up at the demonstration tea ceremony I attended once in college. Sato-sensei offered extra credit to attend, so I did. It was like watching a barista on sedatives, with customers on Ritalin, dressed in sumptuous kimonos. That somehow brought me to the scene in Amélie Nothomb's *Stupeur et tremblements* when she's compelled to eat a white chocolate ball with the *parfum* of Hokkaido melon. The light had waned by then, so I could only make out the features of the comers and goers while their faces were bathed in the artificial light spilling out of the salon along with them. After a blur of traffic, a slender black-haired woman in a cream teddy bear coat and powder pink Stan Smiths turned off the lights and locked up behind herself. I can't remember how I got home. I must have walked all the way because the river of thoughts kept flowing uninterrupted. A metro ride or taxi would've broken the spell. I ran through a mental barre warm-up. I ran through the order of tea by caffeine content, from least to most: tisanes, white teas, green teas, oolongs, black teas. I marvelled at the fact you could leave the order unchanged to map optimal water temperatures from least to most. When I at last swung open the door to my flat, I was startled by the terrifying sight of a cloaked figure in blue mask and gloves -- me, in the mirror I'd put up for last-minute appearance checks before stepping out. Both of us gasped and gave an absurd little jump. I threw my disposable accessories into the trash. Good riddance! My face had pinkish creases stamped into it, like what a chubby baby gets on its thighs from disposable diapers. My hands were damp, with pruney fingerprints as after a too-long hot bath. Maybe someone else would've considered the day a waste, but not Huguette. I was excited to try again tomorrow. Mrs. Tremblay always used to say I was the most tenacious kid she'd ever taught and that made me so proud. In books and movies, it was talent that was re-warded, but in life, it was tenacity. The next day was Thursday. Every fourth Thursday, I pay Yuki a visit for my L.E.D. gel manicure. In truth, my nails start looking a bit fatigued by week three, but the process is pricey, so I hold out another week.

* * *

Now the usually silent male detective speaks up. He is one of those who shaves his head to camouflage baldness, then sports a beard to double down on intentionality. He's wearing a new-looking tweed sports jacket with laughable English gentleman elbow patches over a threadbare knit turtleneck in effortful black. I think he has it reversed: it's the blazer that should be well worn-in and the layer next to his skin that should look fresh and new. Cop chic, I suppose. "Madame, let's not yet proceed to Thursday. Please, to the best of your ability, and in the most detail, walk us through Wednesday night. Did you take a shower when you got home?"

I didn't take a shower. He's forcing me to get into banality, but so be it. I did many things at once, as many people do who live without people or pets to relax and distract them. I tore off my clothes, peeling away each piece into its correct laundry basket-- regular, delicates, or hand wash. Simultaneously, I made a pot of *kukicha*-- that's the less desirable green stems-- and ran a bath full of Epsom salts. I lit a jasmine flower candle. Is it also considered relevant that I skipped dinner and wore my black and white *toile de Jouy* pee-jays? She asks why I didn't eat dinner. "Sorry," I say, "You just touched your face. Do you mind using hand sanitizer before you touch anything else? Thanks." I say that in French to avoid trivializing the interpreter. She pumps twice before looking at me expectantly. I skipped dinner because my appetite had sort of turned off. It does that sometimes; when I've been feasting deliciously, it'll turn on something fierce, but if I go too long without eating, the urge withers like a discouraged erection and hides. I fell asleep with my laptop open next to me in bed, several tabs open relating to

Masahisa. There wasn't much, in fact, nothing personal, just indisputable evidence that he was a master *coiffeur*. The relentless parade of crisp bobs and tousled waves must have lulled me to sleep.

Thursday, I woke up with a sense of purpose. Sure I had no work, but I had something better to do than work. I packed a light picnic for myself, shrugged on a hooded puffer, a new set of blue prophylactic gear (I'd come to think of the color as Blue-19), and headed directly to my bench with a view. I timed my arrival just right. Imagine my joy when I witnessed Masa himself unlocking and illuminating Masa Coupe. He wore the same black nylon I'd seen him in last time. I caught only a glimpse of his profile before he was swallowed up by the doorway, but it was enough to reconfirm the hardness of his handsomeness, a masculinity, asserting itself through his flesh, that sprung from the stone of his soul. He had a long workday, many clients. They entered slouching under the weight of their rice cooker sized handbags, exited heads held high, a victor's posture. I hadn't yet had a good look at his hands, but I fantasized them thick and strong with a paradoxical delicacy, a hummingbird's touch. Later, when I saw them up close, and was caressed by them, I was proven right. Explicit thoughts caused my palms to perspire. I snapped off my Blue-19 gloves, resolving not to touch my face. Jesus only knew what could be on that bench. When snacktime announced itself in my gurgling belly, I rubbed cold, wet sanitizer jelly into my hands, followed by a coat of unctuous hand cream. Inspecting my chapped hands, my heartbeat paused as I recalled my forgotten nail appointment. What was happening to me? I'd nearly missed it.

Yuki would've been worried ... angry? I didn't even know because it had never happened before. I crushed the last of my *tartine* into my mouth and hightailed it to her *atelier* in the seventh. Tucked into a tiny apartment in an unrenovated building facing a stone church and adjacent to a chainsmokers' high school, Chez Yuki is a rather unusual nail place. I would have bet she's lacking a business license, and I sharply suspected there was a futon and all her clothes in the *armoire* behind her workstation. I never would ask if she lived there, and she would never say.

End of February, start of March is the right time to transition from winter reds to spring pinks, or at least I was so informed by Yuki. She's a licensed (and even, in Japan, award winning) color consultant, whose c.v. runs the full spectrum from personal makeovers to color creation for Shiseido. Yuki is far from your average nail tech, Chez Yuki being more like a shrine to color than a workaday salon. As many times as I've been, I always find something to feast my eyes on there. The walls of the main-- and I think only-- room are sponged a deep, bright, streaky magenta, a hue that would assault the eye in a sunny spot, but in the quavering grey light off the Seine, refreshes. We sit on raw silk cushions in a hopeful shade, the color of mandarin peel, the color of luxury branding. Between us, her hands work and mine repose on a low table shiny black as fresh licorice. The flowers in the blue glass vase are always different. The cloud formations in the window are always different. Framed on the wall is a magnificent color chart that I could imagine getting lost in for hours. It's like a stroll garden strewn with monuments to delicate emotions. Fiery Red, Champagne, Night, Billiard, Mignonette, Indigo, Café au Lait, Celadon… each one a daydream-in-waiting. Yuki herself is like a gilded *bonbon*, who creates a certain overall impression with so many little details too numerous to ever notice all at once. There's her rootless blond hair that calls to mind sugared chestnuts, her copper-bronze *ombré* eyeshadow that seems to have seeped out of her eyelids rather than have been dabbed on, the glitter twinkling on her pointed nails with their rosy beds and seamless cuticles. Even her indoor slippers feature some complicated needlepoint that you don't want to stare at for too long, but that fascinate with their implication of labor intensity. If Helena Rubinstein had known Yuki, she would have added to her aphorism, "There are no ugly women, only lazy women," the addendum, "... and ultra-cute women can become unfathomably adorable with a bit of gratuitous work." From hints and snippets here and there, I've gathered that my little nail artist came to France for a love that fell short of expectations. And here she is. Here we all are. I look at the detective spinning a pearl stud in its lobe hole with her right hand. Who knows, maybe it was love that had enticed her onto the police force once upon a time.

Yuki has the gracious habit of preparing for her clients pour-over coffee out of these brown bag-paper ready-to-serve packets with a cartoon chipmunk leaning against a ceramic

mug decorated with an autumn leaf on them.
That day, she served mine in a Paris Saint-
Germain team mug with one Canderel and two
creams beside it on an embroidered napkin so
fine, it could have been a handkerchief. It even
bore a Y monogram. As we sipped, her little
parakeet hopped and twittered in its white wire
cage. "Shhh, Takeshi, shhh."

I tilted toward her and revealed, "I've
met someone."

"Yes?" her eyes opened wide, informa-
tion portholes.

"Someone very, very special."

"Yes?" She'd stopped blinking as
though her pupils were microphones.

I pursed my lips, releasing them into this
bombshell: "He's the most handsome man I've
ever met, so chic, but that's not what draws me
to him."

Yuki discreetly pushed her cup aside,
unconsciously making room for the conjured

man between us. I continued, with a dreamy-determined look in my eye, "It's his spirit. The expression on his face and the beauty he creates with his hands."

"His hands?" Yuki's fingertips sparkled as she turned her hands over, looking at them now as beauty creators and imagining the elegant man who'd won my heart this way.

"He's a master *coiffeur*. He has his own salon with many illustrious clients."

"Really?" Even in French, she says "really" like Japanese, with that lilting pitch of deep incredulity.

"He cuts Brigitte Macron, [my mouth just wouldn't form Carla Bruni], but I really shouldn't have said anything. He keeps her private, off social media and everything." Her glittering hand shot up to her mouth and hovered there, sealing in the speechlessness. "His discretion is one of his most appealing qualities. He doesn't brag. He doesn't boast. He isn't needy like so many men."

"When are you going to see him?" she whispered. I took a long gulp of my cooled coffee and said with finality, "Tonight."

We stared at each other, each lost in a version of tonight. Yuki bit her lip and said quietly, "You want a deeper pink for more impact, not a neutral."

"No," I agreed, "no nudes."

Freshly lacquered beneath my latex gloves, I hurried back to my bench, losing myself in daydreams for hours while I watched the salon door. One thing I like to do is practice writing Japanese characters in my mind, stopping and starting over any time I botch the order of strokes. It's an old habit from my student days, originating with exam study, that now just keeps me from ever getting bored. I always take care to follow the rules of strokes: Horizontal strokes go left to right.

Verticals from top to bottom.

I always begin my practice with basic characters like man, one, and sun, progressing on to more complex ones like wind, after, south. Like this, time never stands still and never drags.

Man, one, sun. Man, one, sun.

Wind, after, south. Wind, after, south.

The light waned and finally, behind my chunky dark lensed glasses, I perceived the nimble form of that fascinating man crossing the threshold, molecules trembling in the open air, becoming one with the evening. Feeling for my hood and my handbag, I hurried after him, maintaining a good distance, the right distance both for the virus and the circumstances. He brought me down into the Metro, that fetid sewer, the one part of Paris that compares un-favorably to its counterpart in Montréal. Lucki-ly, I had my card. Together, but apart, we boarded a train. I was far from the only girl in surgical accessories. A lot of people wore masks and gloves of questionable efficacy, but Masahisa was exposed. He was deep in thought-- his face was still, but his eyes were active, tracking interior movements. Between his feet, he set down on the filthy floor a bulky gym bag by Le Coq Sportif with tricolour straps. I guessed he was leading me to a gym, but it didn't seem prudent. Imagine the surfaces, uncommonly microbial in even the best of times. As we passed familiar stops and left them behind, I started to feel a little queasy regarding our destination. I'd never been to the suburbs, never once, and wouldn't have guessed that he had any business there either. Were there no gyms closer to the salon he could use? Or was the gym bag filled with something else? A sinister presentiment pushed into my veins, pushing the good blood aside. We changed to another line and continued on. My breathing quickened beneath my damp mask when I saw him grip his bag and rise to get off. The *banlieues*, I didn't know one from another, but I trusted that a marvelous person like him had a good reason for every-where he went. Only a handful of passengers got off here, dark men and veiled women, a couple with a sweet child in diminutive track pants. I instinctively edged a little closer to Masa, fearful of losing him. By now, it was fully dark. The street lamps lit only selectively, leaving pools of mystery between them. Just when I thought we couldn't get any further from the Metro without bumping into another station, he abruptly turned off the boulevard onto a narrow, trash-strewn lane. I followed him still. He followed a chain link fence until he came to a small, white sign, the generic, cheaply made kind from another era, from the stores that used to say SIGNS MADE HERE. Beyond that lay a dark doorway recessed behind a dirty welcome mat. I hung back, but my solitariness afforded me a clear view. He dissolved into the doorway. Caught off guard by the abruptness of our separation, I froze. What next? If you've never followed anyone before, it's not clear quite what to do. I approached the white sign to better understand it. The letters, in a chlorinated sky blue, read DOJO NUAGE BLANC. It would have looked nice, classier, if it had the Japanese characters for "white cloud" too, but no. The word "dojo" intimidated me. It's like a shorthand for "getting hurt" and I didn't want to. I reflexively backed away from the door, wanting to go home, terrified now of the night and the vermin who surely rustled their way through these streets. All alone, I peeled off my gloves and mask, stuffing them in my pockets for the return trip. Whether my body or the ambiance, I didn't know, but I felt warm, even hot, and pulled off my hood as I turned the corner onto another side street, looking for a spot where I could wait for him inconspicuously. My hair tumbled over my shoulders, startling every time a breeze touched it. No benches anywhere and I couldn't actually recall the route back to the station and anyway didn't want to miss Masa on the way out, so for lack of something better, I began to circle the block slowly, like a shark swimming, swimming, always past the White Cloud Dojo. To pass the time, I counted my circuits out loud. I'd say "one", "two", whatever number, just as I rounded the first corner past his doorway, not right in front of it, so as not to be caught out when he finally did exit. To shake things up, and keep myself alert, I said every first number in French: *"un"*, every second in English: "two", every third in Japanese: *"san"*. If I made a mistake, and it was hard not to, I had to begin again at one. I mean: *"un"*. I really was starting to wonder how long his karate practice or whatever (judo?) was going to take, when I heard footsteps behind me. I whipped my head around, like an owl, with my wide feet planted on the sooty pavement, scarred with old gum scabs and littered with spent cigarette butts. Two scruffy young men, looking like they'd been paid by Adidas to dress alike, approached me, too fast. I felt sweat bead in my armpits and between my breasts. The shorter one spat at his own feet and blurted, in a bored tone, "*Sale juive*."

Here my embassy guy cuts in, "Dirty Jew."

"Well, I'm not gonna very well say 'dirty Jewess'. That's *their* talk. I just leave it un-translated."

The male detective rifles through his files. "We have the police report from that night here."

My lawyer cuts in, with a solicitous tone, "So you don't need to go through all that again."

The female detective rushes to add, "... though it would be helpful to put it in this new context. How about we break for five and just try to walk us through it for the last time when we return?"

I ask for a coffee I don't really want, just to have something to ask for. I'll walk them through nothing. Thugs and their thuggery, human swine, nothing to do with me. They just wanted to use me for target practice.

Ok, back on stage, with all the cast assembled. My lawyer says in French, making the antsy interpreter roll her eyes, "The attack of which my client was an unfortunate victim bears no relevance on the investigation in which we are currently engaged. In the interest of time, and given that it may be only a matter of weeks or days until gatherings such as this are discouraged in the interest of public health, I urge you, with all cordiality, to move forward."

Now it was the female detective's turn to roll her eyes. (I felt like I was back at the Modern Languages Faculty at UQAM.) She had done something to her hair during the break, but I couldn't discern what. It reminded me of Yvonne and her silk square scarves-- you turn your back for a minute and she's re-knotted it ever so subtly, but you can't tell how, and if you ask her, she'll deny it, fidgeting with one's costuming being one of her cardinal sins. The detective persists in a hectoring tone, "So, you turned around, one of the would-be assailants spat on the ground and said dirty Jewess."

"Yes."

Her guy counterpart cuts in, "But you're not a Jew?"

"No."

"Why do you think they thought you were?"

I say drily, "I don't know what they thought, only what they said."

The lawyer sounds agitated, "She doesn't read minds."

The woman: "Just let her think. Every-thing helps in an investigation. Even theories."

"Especially theories," adds her sidekick.

I'd been mistaken for Jewish before, in Montréal, so I could guess, even if my guess was only based on past stupidities. I'd had a fourth-grade teacher who was an open anti-semite, not that unusual.

"Umm," I feel like a puppet run by an imbecile, "because I have red hair?" They all look at me. It seems like I'm supposed to haz-ard more guesses, so I continue, "I'm zaftig and I have a Roman nose. In fact, French-Canadians and Eastern European Jews have the two highest rates of redheads of all world groups." National Geographic lesson thus complete, I fold my hands in my lap, where my pink nails still look surprisingly fresh given all they've seen.

That night, terror had invaded every cell of my body, making each one tremble to the point of liquefaction. "I'm not Jewish," I said in my weird accent, years of efforts at elocution melting away, "but you," plural you, "are Coronavirus carrying Arabs. Do you even wash your hands after you shit?" The passive one had looked on wide eyed, his mouth open and glistening in the lamplight, while the active one had lunged forward and grabbed a thick handful of my hair.

"Fat whore," he'd breathed out in a cloud of halitosis that made me wince worse than the pain in my scalp.

"Yeah, you bet I'm fat," I'd laughed, "that's why I'll survive the virus and you won't. Malnourished limp-dicks like you," singular, familiar you, "will be the first to expire in their hospital beds. You'll be begging a Jew in a lab coat to save you." He'd made me angry and I'd been hungry and tired. The combo makes me aggressive. Before they could make a move or even formulate a *bon mot*, a tall man, broadly built, shades darker than them, with roots further south, stepped out of a black patch, brandishing a knife.

"Leave her!" he shouted. They froze, considering his obvious superiority, even if he was alone. "Get out of here, shit," he added in a softer, disappointed tone. The copper clump of my hair dropped. The two sprinted off like rats. "Everything ok, Mademoiselle? Uh, Madame?"

"Mademoiselle, Monsieur. I'm okay. You're a hero."

"Not at all, no hero, just a man compelled to be neighbors with these aspiring criminals." He, the hero whose name turned out to be Pierre, had driven me home, mercifully not asking what I was doing there, declining a cash reward either out of dignity, gallantry, or fear of contagion.

I took a boiling shower, downed a pot of jasmine black despite the hour, and revived. I visited the dojo's website, where the street address showed me where I'd been and the schedule gave me an idea of how I could orchestrate another meeting with Masahisa. He was so far blissfully ignorant of how much I'd suffered for him. The next day, I'd walked into my local precinct and filed a report, with the full understanding that there'd be no follow up.

The detective man says, "Yes, we have here the report and we even managed to locate Monsieur Valentine, Pierre, who corroborates this account. He says it was about nine o'clock when he left you at your front door. Does that sound about right?"

"That's it."

"And is it right that you returned to the same exact spot the very next evening?"

"Yes, that's right." The detectives exchange obvious glances, while my lawyer and interpreter guard impassive expressions.

What? I'm crazy? No, not crazy, just in love.

Dojo Nuage Blanc had a homemade website in illegible blue and white-- I get it, clouds in the sky-- that told me next to nothing. It was in French, but peppered with so much obscure Japanese vocab of the type you never get in school. I had to cross-reference every-thing with the glossary from the well done site of a better-looking dojo in Brussels. They have names for every little thing, not all of it worth looking up, a lot of little studs, a lot of shrine components, several ways to stare and shout. This place was confusing; it seemed to teach a bunch of different martial arts. In the movies I'd endured with nerd-boys in college, a training hall had one master, in one discipline. This spot was all over the place, with a jumbled schedule of different styles, like one of those dance studios where they swiftly lift the tempo-rary barre from the Ballet Débutant class and whisk it away for the Parcours Avancé. I was clicking around, trying to make heads or tails of it, believe me not easy-- you clicked on an instructor's name and sometimes got a verbose bio and photo of breaking a brick on a sunset beach, and sometimes got absolutely nothing. The place promised to be huge inside because classes happened simultaneously, further complicating my job. While Masa was inside, and I was being attacked, there were several possibilities for what he was learning (or teaching-- I could see him in a black belt, leading others on The Way.) Both options, though, had to be cross-referenced with the Belgian glossary. As I was wading through the murk of it, Yvonne called, her lovely voice cutting through my concentration. "Huguette, my dear, your generation is usually ignorant of the natural remedies, so I'm calling to tell you, jot this down, and go immediately, first thing tomorrow, as soon as the shops open, to the biological store, and get these herbs, dried from the bulk jars. You will follow to the letter this recipe, don't deviate by a gram, and you'll blend it and store in a glass receptacle. Glass, never plastic."

"Hi, Yvonne, thanks for calling. What is this? What am I making?"

"Oh," her breathing became embarrassed, "it's a tisane for pulmonary health. To see you safely through this crisis. Do you have a pad and pencil? Write it exactly. One hundred grams of mint. Yes? I'll go on. One hundred grams eucalyptus. Right. Fifty grams elderberry, not to be confused with elderflower. Okay. Twenty-five grams of ground ginger. Finally one hundred grams linden. Do I need to repeat it?"

"No, I got it."

"Good, boiling water, long steep, twice a day, morning and night. This will reduce mucus in the lungs, promoting resistance to viral infections."

"Thanks. You're a good friend, Yvonne."

"You are too." We said goodbye after lamenting the closure of the dance studio. But it would only be for a couple of weeks.

Why is it that whenever one is most absorbed in research, that's exactly when everyone calls? Just as I'd turned my attention back to teasing out the tangled threads of this crazy schedule, with its "open practice" and "pedagogy" in all these different styles of I don't know what, I was pestered by the insistent FaceTime ring. My sister. I tapped on. "Hi Coralie," I said in my sullen sister voice.

She wasted no time. "See? I told you, you should have stayed here. You know France is gonna be ravaged by the China Flu."

"The China Flu? Are you gonna pay royalties to the nineteenth century?"

"Ha ha, seriously Huguette, you ought to be home. We've only got like two cases in the whole province." Coralie's homely nasal whine made me even a little nostalgic for Québec, the way she opened her mouth wide on the second syllable of "province". She had no idea what she sounded like, though, and was neither proud nor ashamed of her accent, just enjoyed the oblivious, satisfied complacency of those who stay home. I thought I was thinking to myself that it's ironic that in our family, it wasn't the pretty one who moved away to a glamourous, foreign city, but the book-nerd one, but then Coralie butt in, "Why ironic? It's not like you spend your nights sipping champagne on the deck of the boat of a male model turned river pilot named Maximillian, and I'm home in my Roots sweatpants ordering in jalapeño poutine." I must have spoken out loud. That's a habit I've been trying to break since forever. It embarrassed me so much over the years, in all different contexts; it was almost a relief when, in JAP 101, sweet, little Sato-sensei mistook it for a cultural thing: "Yuu-getto-san [that's how she pronounced Huguette], in Japan, ladies don't whisper their thoughts while interlocutor speaks."

I snapped back into my conversation with my sister, "Indeed, indeed. I only wish somewhere here did take out jalapeño poutine. Then Paris would really live up to its reputation!" We laughed together, like when we were little girls in matching dresses. "Listen, Coco. Stay safe, your peeps too. I'll do the same-- obsessive hand washing. *Pas de bises, d'accord*? Love you."

"Love you, Huguie."

I dove right back into my project. I flipped over to the blank side of Yvonne's tisane recipe and copied down, phonetically, like a monkey, the course names:
KENDO BEGINNER / KENDO INTERMEDI-
ATE+ / FREE KEIKO / KENDO KATA
IAIDO MUSO SHINDEN RYU / IAIDO MUSO
JIKIDEN EISHIN RYU

Beneath the schedule were all sorts of arcane prerequisites, like you could only go to "free keiko" (whatever that was sounded liberating and fun) if you'd already done twelve weeks of "kendo intermediate+" (kendo I already knew from seeing a club practice in the university gym-- weirdos in cage masks), which you could only start after eight weeks of "kendo beginner". Fair enough, but other italicized fine print directives were vague, like you could only do "iaido muso shinden ryu" if you regularly went to "kendo kata", but it was strongly rec-ommended, but not obligatory, to take "iaido muso jikiden eishin ryu" at the same time. I re-read the schedule with an eye toward narrow-ing down what Masahisa had been doing that terrible night. I hoped that way to avoid having to research every term on the schedule. Every evening Monday to Saturday and nothing on Sundays... h'mmm, here we go... ok, Masa was necessarily at either the Iaido Muso Shinden Ryu or Free Keiko. Now re-reading the rules, I saw that I was unqualified to go to either, but that I could come in fresh off the street for Kendo Beginner, that very night. Perfect. My hands still trembled and my scalp still ached from the attack, but what better way to move on than to start a new endeavour? Plus, until my dance class restarted, I needed a sport. There was a very provisional looking red banner scrolling above the schedule announcing that for the time being, the dojo was still open and to please refrain from attending if you were feeling under the weather. Game on!

I arrived to the familiar rusty doorway that now resonated with both menace and promise, fifteen minutes early, as advised by the FAQ's. It felt forbidden but fated, like certain actions in dreams. The door was locked. I pressed a video bell button and was buzzed in without question. I guess I look harmless. The interior was cavernous, with cheap, cold lighting, red and black checkerboard faded linoleum floors, a general Asbestos n' Lead look.   I was trying to figure out what it must've been originally, maybe a small factory? Or a school of some kind? -- and thought I was just thinking, but maybe I was thinking out loud again, because a female voice behind me said, in an accent that made me flash on the Italian Riviera, palm trees and bathtub warm sea, "They used to make frozen pizzas here. No ovens, just a walk-in freezer." I stared at this surprise. A petite woman, shorter than me, of child-bearing but non-specific age, in the kind of indigo tie-on clothes I sold everyday, with a long, thick, tight plait of repressed platinum blond waves resting over one shoulder. Her deep set eyes would have been beady if not a pale Swarovski blue. Her lips were injected mercilessly, making her straight, pointy nose look a shade too shrunken. Overall, Japanese Fencing Barbie, not something you see every-day, or even imagine. It felt like I was seeing something I wasn't supposed to; this was reserved for dojo members; I was meant to walk by her on the street in her Louboutins and roll my eyes at the predictable Chanel chain bag. I swallowed hard, then meekly choked on my words, " I... I'm here for the beginner class. It's my first time here."

"I know. You American or something?"

"Sort of, no, yeah. *Québécoise.*"

"Yeah, exactly. You have yoga clothes or something?"

"Sort of, yeah, no. My ballet stuff. The website said--"

"I know," she cocked her head like a little squirrel, "follow me. You can get changed. No one else is coming. I have no other beginners and my teaching assistant is quarantining himself after a tournament in Korea." She showed me to a dingy locker room that must once have hosted the frozen pizza ladies. "When you're dressed, meet me in the small studio. The door on the left."

I haltingly got changed, with that sense of vulnerability and disorientation one always feels in an unknown locker room. When I padded silently, in my pink leather ballet shoes, to the door on the left, my eyes jolted at the change of ambiance. This space was roomily intimate, just small enough to be called "the small studio", I guess, but large enough to host sport. It looked like it had been lifted by a crane out of an entirely other building, though what I couldn't picture, just not here. It was lit with dim incandescent bulbs giving off a warm golden glow. The walls were panelled in dark wood, the floors covered in tatami mats edged in a black, red, and gold floral jacquard. Racks of sticks, maybe poles, and swords (it looked like) were mounted on one wall. The opposite wall had a miniature Shinto shrine (that was for sure, immediately recognizable) surrounded by various *objets d'art*: folded paper decorations, a bonsai tree (I assumed *faux*, where would it get light?, but who knows) potted in a blue and white porcelain pot (beautiful, just my taste), small raw wooden boxes, maybe some figurines, or no, incense burners, not sure, that my gaze touched without ingesting. She was sitting on her feet beside and under all that, her back to it. I stepped in, instinctively ducking into a semi-bow.

"Take those off. We practice barefoot."

I waved my hand, ashamed, at my black leotard and pink tights. "Oh, I... my feet will still be covered."

She didn't seem to have it in her to smile or reassure, "It's fine for today. You don't have to worry about foot fungus. These mats are synthetic. I spray them often." I nodded, not really knowing what she was talking about. I could see this would be one of those introductory lessons where I would always be stumbling to catch up. It would take several minutes before I realized that tatami mats are generally made of reeds, like in Kurosawa films, and that maybe those harbor foot fungus.

Monkey see, monkey do usually works for me. I lowered myself to sit on my feet too, but facing the wrong direction. I turned around.

"This is your first time?"

"Yes."

"First time learning kendo or any martial art?"

"Any." I thought she would next ask me why I'd come, but she didn't.

"What's your name?"

"Huguette." A flicker of a smile, like she might have found my name funny.

"Iris, but you call me Sensei." I flashed on Sato-sensei, who occasionally would bake pink-iced bunny-shaped brownies to share with us. "Kendo is the way of the sword. The sword is the less important part. The hardest thing to learn is how to be on the Way. You fall off and then you get back on." I'd always found this Zen bullshittery so pretentious, but it seemed like it was going to be the price of admission to Masa's world. "Don't worry so much about learning. The movements and the connections will come later. For now, just imitate." That I can do, I work in fashion after all. In fact, I think Shizuka may have spoken those exact words when she hired me. My first week, I wasn't allowed to touch a single kimono or piece of knitwear. I had to just follow her around, making note of what she hung where, what she folded how. I was allowed to dust with feathers on a pole. The wall mounted Japanese schoolgirl backpacks were hard to reach.

Iris-sensei gave me a *faux* sword that she ripped out of its plastic wrap like a candy bar. "Bamboo," she said, then added, without irony, "but you see it as sharp steel and treat it like an extension of your mind." I had to bite my tongue not to giggle, and pay extra attention not to think out loud. I imitated venerating it, bowing, stroking. Then it was time to pick it up. Easier said than done. She found fault with my grip-- right hand over left-- over and over again until the whole hour had passed. It was over and I was glad. I hadn't had a minute of fun. After the second bookending round of stroking and bowing, I made to get up, but her hand shot out. "Not before me." I awkwardly trailed her to the changing room. It looked even more squalid after the minimalist chic of the studio. Without a word, she turned her back to me and stripped off her dark blue cotton with brisk, fast gestures. Her back was exceptionally thin and narrow; each vertebra cast its own shadow. Under the fluorescent light, her white, semi-translucent skin looked sickly, but I knew it as the type that would photograph beautifully under the right conditions. I slowly peeled off my dancewear, hiding my rolls as a matter of habit, or principle, though there was no one looking. One could feel there was no danger of her suddenly whipping around to steal a glance or ask a question. One could sense that firmly turning her back on others was in her nature. I couldn't tear my eyes away as she slipped into a black mesh thong and matching underwire (probably Cosabella). I felt my mouth drop open as she gingerly stepped into a black Swiss dot mesh garter belt and deftly attached it to a pair of nude stockings, also dotted in black (It would have been too matchy-matchy if visible on the street.) that she tore savagely from a new Cervin pack. They looked to be about fifteen *denier*, too light for the season and so fragile, she'd be lucky to get another use out of them. Over that, she added a black lambskin pencil skirt and white button down blouse (I'd stake my life on Anne Fontaine, but just maybe Rayure). She undid her hair and it sprung out like a jack-in-the-box into an elongated, chaotic halo. Having packed her things into a duffel, tightly like a parachute, she slipped into a pair of sensible suede pumps, with a square seven-centimetre heel and a high instep. She clearly planned to

walk. Last of all, she shrugged into a black nylon trench with a reflective triangle on the back.
I'd seen that before. Looking down to confirm I
was dressed-- I was-- I risked, "Where did you
buy that rain jacket? I'd love one just like it."
She turned to face me, her swollen lips shel-
lacked with a fresh coat of pink gloss I'd never
even seen her apply, too shiny, and looked at
me with either disdain or pity. Maybe she'd
been hoping for a Zen riddle or just for me to
respect the silence.

"No idea. It's my husband's."

"Maybe you could ask him for me."

"No one sees him now, during Fashion
Week."

"Oh, does he work in fashion?"

"Hair."

"Oh," I said, trying to funnel my shock at
her as Masa's wife into a mild interest in her

association with a hairdresser. "That must be a handy arrangement for maintaining your color."

"This is natural," she deadpanned.

I smiled, showing I got the joke, but she just said, "When you're ready, I'll lock up behind us."

After a dispiriting gloved and masked journey on the paranoid metro, I started a pot of Lapsang Souchong, whose caffeine would sharpen my thoughts, whose smoky perfume would burn away the indelible torment of Iris in her Helmut Newton element. The first thing I did after my first sip was to go back to the White Cloud schedule to figure out how soon I could go back. Tomorrow evening was Kendo Kata. It was neither clear to me exactly what it was ("kata" means form, but so what?) nor if I was allowed to take it. I probably could have asked her through the Contact form, but that would just give her the chance to say no, so I didn't. It was already late, but knowing that

Yvonne was a night owl, and wanting to tell her that Masahisa had gotten my number from Shizuka and boldly invited me out for a glass of champagne, I dialled her mobile, figuring that she'd have silenced it if she'd gone to bed. It rang only once before an unfamiliar voice answered with, "Hello, it says Huguette?" The voice was older, from the landline era. "Who is this?" A presentiment of bad tidings washed over me.

"This is Yvonne's friend, Huguette," I enunciated each word. Each word scraped my palate a little.

The old voice broke out sobbing, wherever she was. "Oh, it's awful, horrible! The shit of this life! The unfairness!"

"What happened, Madame? Tell me." We'd fallen into the polite "you" routine that's *de rigeur* here and hardly remembered back home.

"Who are you?" she asked again with a touch of hysteria. Remember the Japanese denim brand HYSTERIC GLAMOUR? I used to love it, as a sillier Fiorucci Safety Denim.

"I'm Yvonne's friend. From ballet class." I felt fear.

"Oh, my dear, how to say it? Yvonne's dead."

"No, she's not," I blurted.

"A heart attack, my dear, the heart."

"Wait, what?"

"She died of a heart attack."

"I don't think so."

"What a shock, my dear. I'm very, very sorry."

"Who are you, Madame?" I looked around my room desperately, eyes hunting for something to see.

"I'm Marie, her ex-sister-in-law. She must have listed me somewhere as an emergency contact."

"Marie. Oh. I wanted to tell her, I made love to a beautiful Japanese man."

"What's that, dear? Could you speak more slowly? You have an accent."

"When's the funeral?"

"I'm still arranging that, my dear. I'm sorry for you. I'll call you when it's clear. I have your number here. Good day."

I walked around in circles, muttering to myself for a while. By the time I remembered my Lapsang Souchong, it tasted like a worn pair of wellies. I dumped the contents of the pot into the kitchen sink. The swollen brown leaves clung to the drain, clinging in turn to my fingers as I tried to clear them into the trash. They wouldn't let go. I scraped them away and then there they still were, a kaleidoscope of compost on my pink painted nails. Tears dripped down my cheeks. Instead of wiping them away, I sidled over to the front door mirror, pretty confident I wouldn't make a mess; the tea paste still clung to me like metal filings to a magnet. Why are reflections of our own crying faces so gratifying? It's a bunch of factors: the liberation from the expectation of prettiness, the novelty of transformation, the surprise at the efficiency of the tear and snot production, and the poignant beauty of it all. The tears magnified and glorified individual pores as they shimmied down my face, tremulous spotlights. As my hands air dried, clusters of tea began dropping off onto the floor. I sank along with them, plopping down onto the floor. It had been a year ago almost to the day that Yvonne and I had taken our first and only trip together. The idea got started when I'd mentioned that I'd never been outside Paris.

Yvonne had done an incredulous double take.

"You've never seen France?"

"Uh-uh. Just Versailles and it was enormously crowded with school trip groups and Chinese tourists."

"Yes," she tutted, "it can take on the aspect of a Louis Vuitton *entrepôt*." I had shrugged and smiled because there is something loveable about those tiny, glossy haired visitors. Not the ones who cut their eyelids and file down their jaws, but the natural ones, with shapely calves and moon faces. Yvonne had animated so fast, I'd startled, almost jumping.

"Listen, my little *coquette*. We are going to pack our weekend bags. We are going to get on a TGV. We are going to check into a little *chambre d'hôte*. We are going to visit a truly elegant *château,* not the circus at Versailles. And we're going to do it all now, in the low season, when prices are low and crowds are sparse. I won't take no for an answer."

I'd never done anything like that before. The idea had excited me. I'd seen a segment on the TGV. It was like an airplane on tracks, faster even than the Japanese bullet train.

"Then I won't give no for an answer."

What is better than packing a weekend bag? It must be the peak of any trip. You project your mind twenty-four, forty-eight, seventy-two hours into the future, and plugging in variables of weather and happenstance, you summon the hours of trip to the surface of your skin. Shamanism. I hadn't done it in ages, though I'd studied plenty of tutorial graphics in the fashion magazines. I knew a good, high quality bag was essential. I didn't have one, but I knew who did.

There's an old, probably formerly charming lecher in the apartment next door. He goes away frequently; I know each time because he pays me to water his plants. He talks about his plants like people. That one sympathetic trait, plus the fact that he seems genuinely attracted to me, is his saving grace. At a time when I heard him rustling through our shared wall, I re-tied my blue and white cotton *yukata*, gingko motif, tight around my midsection, stepped into my bronze leather home Birkenstocks, and tiptoed into the hall to ring his doorbell. The rustling moved from our wall to behind the front door, became fumbling with locks until the door opened with a trepid slowness. I arranged my face to look as friendly as possible. "Hello, Alain."

"Aha!" he snapped his fingers. "It's the neighbor from the snows across the sea!" He stroked his white beard and smoothed his eyebrows down, both at one time, with the index and thumb of one hand.

"How are you, Alain?"

"Quite well, quite well. I'd invite you in, but I haven't tidied up."

"Yes, I won't be long. Sorry to disturb."

"Not at all, not at all. A pleasure. This is the first time I realize you paint your toes with the same bewitching red as your hands."

I laughed, hopefully not derisively, as one red-tipped hand flew up to double check that the robe was tightly closed. I looked over his shoulder at the healthy clump of jungle I'd misted so many times. "I was wondering... well, I'm going away this weekend and was wondering if you wouldn't mind lending me a weekend bag? You have such nice ones."

"Canvas or leather?"

"What do you think?"

He stroked his beard again. "Me? I like to see a woman with the leather, but it's as you like."

Seated across from Yvonne on the train, black leather weekender tucked snug in the overhead rack, chocolate chip whole wheat stick on the fold out tray table in front of me, I watched the station, the city, its outskirts, and

the countryside sprint away from me like a joy-
ous child. The carriage's interior was dour.
Everyone was thinking about something different; in the silent cacophony of their thoughts,
one felt overwhelmed. Yvonne was as much at
ease as if she'd been in her dressing gown at
home. "The pleasure, my little *coquette*, is all
in the planning," she explained in her pedagog-
ical voice, dropping a stack of brochures and
laminated maps on her own tray table. She
rode with the direction of travel, me against it.
She'd chosen the configuration-- now it was
like watching her in a tutorial video. "The
Dutch, the Dutch you know, always publishing
this or that study, they've proven that most of
the happiness in anything lies in the anticipation, not the doing."

"It's all mental," I said, quoting Mrs.
Tremblay. "Sharing is caring."

"What, darling?"

"Sorry, just thinking out loud."

"Was that English?"

"Yes, it's a rhyme from kindergarten. *Sharing is caring*. It means sharing is a true expression of love."

"So it is!"

"Yes, want half my chocolate chip stick? The flour's biological."

We'd arrived to Amboise at a midday so grey, you'd think night was upon you. The Loire flowed sluggishly out the windows of our semi-disheveled, but still refined guest house. In the lobby, really a living room, where we had a pot of black tea, English style, and brittle butter cookies, a sporty, tanned blonde let her baby, a boy with gigantic blue eyes of arresting beauty, crawl around the floor rug until he got stuck between the wall and a *setée* and howled like an animal. She scooped him up and scurried upstairs. The *château* was impressive; too big for my field of vision, it belonged on the cover of a book. As I was turning back from being awed by it, I'd noticed her pop a small pill into her mouth. Since she was obviously trying to hide it, I'd refrained from asking about it, but the incident had come back to me immediately after I'd learned of her death. Those must have been heart pills and perhaps she'd known about her broken heart for a long while. We'd ended up touring all the castles in the rain, the most poetic and cinematic way to see them. I was in heaven with the raindrop stippled moats, the mist cloaked towers, the pebbles on the footpaths gleaming like jewels. A bizarre thing happened at the hedge maze at Chenonceau. I can't resist a labyrinth. Yvonne didn't want to go in; it made her nervous. She didn't like the sensation of her body lost in space and time. "The Valley of Kings was built in the age of cruelty," she added with flair. She told me to meet her in the cafeteria, which sold carafes of local wine. These were the days before the lucky Armour Lux, when I wore an old, box cut waxed jacket I'd borrowed from a boyfriend at university and never returned. It had holes in the lining of both hand pockets (which I'd discovered, forgotten about, then discovered again over the years, in a series of enraging sequences of placing an object in my pocket for safekeeping, or especially to keep it dry, only to have it gleefully, spitefully spit out, water slide style, into the muck below). I had to cram everything into the breast pockets, whose ungainly flaps then wouldn't flatten and made my silhouette lumpy on top of boxy. And remember that it was never the high quality genuine British article to begin with, always a Canadian approximation. And remember too that it had never been re-waxed in all the years I'd known it. So picture me, in this jalopy of a jacket, holding an umbrella aloft that was black on the outside, blue sky Magritte-ish print on the underside, heading into the maze in this tourist-repellent weather. The rain has transitioned from mist to sheets and the charm is waning.

The silence is near mystical, how I imagine life on a submarine, a silence buried deep in the omnipresence of water. My first step in crunched the gravel startlingly; I wouldn't have thought it so easily disturbed. I continued through, crunch crunch crunch crunch, for I don't know how long, with an increasing solitude. The castle visitors, conspicuously absent the Chinese, and the staff, forbidding in their masks and gloves, felt a continent away. They were dry, snug between wall tapestries; their feet danced on a black and white checkerboard; audio guide voices murmured in their ears in their native tongues. To them, the Loire was a view through a window. To me, it was the master of the storm clouds, the curtains of rain, the improvised rivulets running over imperceptible slopes. I could feel its rush in my ears, where two minuscule labyrinths stayed impenetrable. A voice cut through the quiet like a guillotine. "Hello? Hello?" I jumped out of my skin and must have yelped because the female voice added, "Sorry to disturb your solitude, but I need some assistance." Spinning on my axis, I could only see bushes. From that one sentence, I could hear geography and entitlement. Had I really come all this way over rail lines and through the centuries to do a favor for a *parisienne* who could do it herself? "Where are you?" I asked warily. We both burst out laughing. What a question. "Ok," I said, "just keep talking and I'll try to follow your voice."

"What should I talk about?"

"Doesn't matter." I'd already walked into one dead end and was doing a robot u-turn to pursue another route. "You could sing something."

"What should I sing?" She giggled.

"Whatever you want." I seemed to be getting closer to her. "Whatever you'd pick first at a karaoke bar."

"A karaoke bar. Never been. You're not French. Let me guess, are you from Louisiana?"

I was indeed closer. She sounded like she was no more than a meter away, as the crow flies. "Close. Québec."

She giggled again, "Only a continent away."

"It's the same continent. Different people though." I turned the corner and saw her before she saw me. Her back was to me, as her wheelchair was wedged in a shallow declivity that had become a ditch in the alluvial onslaught. My first impression of her, the one you always recall most clearly, was of the narrow cut shoulders of her black leather jacket and the undisturbed line of her blunt bob, a solid block of chestnut. She held a clear plastic umbrella piped in black. She turned just her head around and peered at me like an owl on a branch. "Hi!"

"Hello," I answered, trying to keep the daze out of my voice.

"Yes, I'm in a wheelchair. And you have a lot of red hair."

"Here we are. Tell me what to do."

"It's really a matter of brute force. Would have been better if a man had come along."

"That's so often true, huh?" That made her giggle again.

"Yeah. You need to engage your core and your thigh muscles and push and tilt this damn chair at the same time." I attempted that, grunted a little, but it didn't budge. She apologized. The apology made me feel so bad, I was motivated to try harder so she wouldn't have to say it again. I inhaled, held my breath, pushed it down toward my pelvis, visualized dislodging that wheel from the mud, exhaled, and-- yes-- I'd jostled her out on my own. We cheered together. I swung her chair around and stood in front of her. "Do you want me to push you?" She shook her head. For the first time, I could get a long, hard look at her. I was punished for it. She was, I saw, threateningly beautiful: clear skin draped tight over a symmetrical skull, wide-set eyes under dark brows, exclusive nostrils, flawless teeth inside a mouth discreetly painted a matte peony pink. Even seated, she was imposingly tall. Semi-sheer charcoal stockings stretched out over long bones that could have belonged to another species; her shins would have made good femurs. She had her relentless legs folded at that angle the tall adopt in Economy Class, that posture that works like a quiet snapped finger to bring a flight attendant rushing over with Business level service. The hands folded in her lap had the unvarnished nails of a woman too interesting to get her nails done. My eyes caught on her heeled shoes. I was trying to decide if they could be comfortable, when she pushed me out of my reverie.

"If you step aside, I'll push myself." Oh. I gave a little shrug and moved next to her. "Sorry if I was brusque. I've become used to people getting in my way and not noticing. Do you plan to continue in or try to get out?"

"You?" She already fascinated me more than the landscaping.

She raised a ringless hand to push her hair behind one ear, saying, "I'm going to retrace my route and leave the way I came. I've had enough."

I reflected her wan smile back at her. "Me too. Mind if I accompany you?" I walked at a diagonal from her, since the height of her umbrella kept hitting me painfully when I approached. We made slow progress in the pouring rain, which, if anything, had even picked up intensity. "How did you end up in a wheelchair?" I blurted.

She laughed at me. Yes, definitely not with me.

"I didn't end up this way." She laughed some more, not very charitably. "It's only for a few more months."

"Oh."

She cut in deeper, "You sound a little disappointed. Don't be."

"No, I... I, uh..."

"I'm just kidding! Sorry." She beamed a gorgeous, even smile at me.

"I'm sorry, I just, uh..."

"No, stop. It's me. The chair's made me bitter. Or maybe brought out my real self." She sure liked to laugh at her own jokes. "I had surgery on both knees at once. This is how you recover, apparently."

"Sorry to see that."

"It was my own fault for skiing too ag-gressively. You know telemark?" I could have said, "I'm Canadian," but instead I fell in single file behind her and we processed in silence back to the ingress. As we emerged onto the main path leading to the castle moat, the rain turned off abruptly like a faucet and the sun glazed the whole scene. My companion put on a large pair of tortoiseshell dark glasses and tucked her umbrella into a wire basket attached to her chair.

"Hey," I said timidly, "my friend Yvonne is waiting at the café. Would you like to join us for a coffee?"

Surprise visited her face for a second, then left. "Sure, if I'm not intruding."

Yvonne, true to form, missed not a beat before getting a third glass to go with the carafe of *rosé* she'd been patiently babysitting. Amazing self-control on that woman. She also had an untouched *charcuterie* plate that she slid toward our surprise guest. Nibbling a gherkin, she drew out the whole life story I'd failed to investigate on my own. Our new friend's name was Isabelle. She was from

Grenoble, but now lived in Strasbourg, where she worked as a tax attorney. She'd been married to a cruel Alsatian man, had no children, and soon divorced. She'd come to tour the Loire by herself to try and cheer up after her double knee surgeries, which had left her depressed. She'd also bought herself a white diamond Chaumet twist ring as a get-well-soon present. She was going to pick it up from the jeweller as soon as she got home. She planned to train for an alpine marathon as soon as the doctors gave their approval. Yvonne nodded and murmured approvingly with each nugget. I seethed, as a rule hating attractive female lawyers as well as already tall women who insist on wearing high heels. Isabelle had been much more likeable stuck in the mud. Sitting in a sunbeam, a stemmed glass in her delicate-wristed hand, she'd become tiresome. Just as I was formulating a defense against Yvonne's inevitable gracious invitation for her to come dine with us in Amboise-- she'd already dropped a crumb of praise for the excellent *apéritif* promises of our innkeeper-- Isabelle looked past me at something over my shoulder, her eyes widening in what looked like fear or panic. Yvonne's face did the opposite, contracting into an inquisitive squint. I turned around slowly, bracing myself for whatever sight was about to contort my face in some way. Standing next to the self-service dessert table was a small, faded woman in a Lacoste *piqué* polo tucked into belted hiking trousers. At quick glance, I could count at least three pairs of glasses on or hanging from her person. The *crèmes caramels* beside her looked excellent. Towering at her other side was a young man, the bodybuilder type, in skinny cut jeans almost edging toward a jegging, with his own *piqué* polo untucked, hinting at the splendid torso beneath. This odd couple was striding toward our table with an air of wronged purpose. The woman, whose grey streaked hair was pulled back in a messy bun, was repeat-

ing, "Catherine, Catherine", while the man kept

his sharp jaw firmly set. I whipped back

around to see Isabelle nibbling her cuticles.

The two stumbled around the extra chair we'd

moved half into the aisle to make room for the

wheelchair to roll up to the table. "Catherine,

finally! We were searching everywhere for you.

Everywhere!" Isabelle studied her own hands

without a response. I was dumbstruck, but

Yvonne began, "Excuse me, but will--?"

"Madame, is this woman bothering

you?"

"Bothering? What is--?"

The man furiously texted, shaking his

head, but saying nothing. His partner lunged

forward, picked up Isabelle's glass and sniffed

it. "Alcohol," she said in a disappointed voice

and set it down on the furthest corner of the

tabletop. Continuing as if we didn't exist, she

went on, staring hard at Isabelle as though

struggling to contain fury, "Do you know, Catherine, that fifteen people are waiting for you, all hungry, all expected for lunch, and a dozen others have been mobilized to hunt for you, all worried? Philippe only now called off the search."

"I'm sorry," mumbled Isabelle. Then she mumbled the same thing to us, reaching down to un-brake her wheels. I sat dumbstruck and Yvonne sputtered questions as our erstwhile friend left with her keepers.

* * *

The White Cloud page said that the first class was free. Did that mean only the first-first, yesterday's Kendo Beginner? Or all the firsts of each genre, also today's Kendo Kata? I thought hard, too, about what to wear. Short of a uniform, there was no perfect thing, but something more unisex, more *sportif*, was called for, like grey sweats. I didn't own any grey sweats, any Le Coq Sportif. What a pity. I packed my just laundered ballet garb with disappointed hands. I'd ask about a uniform that night. My disappointed hands fought a tremor whenever Yvonne came into my mind. I tried to push her aside. Life is for the living. Life is for lovers. I needed to focus on coming closer to my dear Masa. I bathed extra careful-ly, exfoliating the soles of my feet, scrubbing my scalp and my ears. When I finally met him, I'd smell like pink grapefruit, not Coronavirus.

With hours yet left to kill before my lesson, I stood in front of the bookshelf, running my fingertips back and forth over the spines of the small Japanese Studies section. I'd re-sold all my other textbooks every semester, but these I'd collected. I remembered, only in outline, a Mishima story we'd read in Post-War Literature, that must have been about kendo. Yes, almost certainly, it was set in a kendo dojo. Where was it? All the Mishima was together in chronological order. Ah, yes. One of my favorites, the white paperback with the dewy red rose that drips blood on the cover. I hadn't handled this book since my things had been cleared by Customs. My books were the first thing I'd unpacked and rearranged. Even then, I'd only placed it on the shelf, not opened it. Now as I thumbed its pages, I saw that they had yellowed, but it had retained its seductive air. Names taken at random intrigued: Zen Master Daigaku, Mibu, Hatakeyama, The Professor. Who were these characters? That's what I love about books. I'd forgotten them, and they'd never know me, but I could meet them again any time I want. The third story in the table of contents was *Sword*. It obviously had to be the one. Oh yes. I love this elegant translation. Already by the middle of the first page, the whole scene has you by the wrists. "One noticed him immediately on entering the dojo. His body and his alone, seemed enveloped in a kind of stillness that arose from the absolute economy of each position he assumed." That's more than a character. It's a magic ghost. I decided, and even wrote myself a note, that if this Coronavirus idleness dragged on any longer, I'd get the original and sit down with my giant, old dictionary and get through it stroke by stroke. I'd also need to download from somewhere the audio, to know how it sounds, very different and possibly very better. Even the title would be better untranslated: *Ken* sounds much more like a sword than "sword" does. The hard, cutting k-sound drops down on the mouth, while the hissing s sounds like it's scared of hurting anyone. Truth be told, I'd already red-penned several words on the first page, correcting, for instance, "hall" to "dojo" ("hall" evokes too much a corridor. If I'd wanted to avoid exotic terms, I'd at least have gone for "training hall" to call to mind the specificity of the room.) and "pleated kimono skirt" to "hakama". The words "pleated" and "skirt" anywhere near each other in a Japanese context, even with another word in between them, just force your brain to see a schoolgirl uniform, tainting whatever machismo is fighting its way out. Naturally, I had to pull my *Tale of Genjis* off the shelf too, all four of them artifacts of the best course I ever took, Comparative Genjis. An advanced level course taught by a notoriously tough professor, Dr. Hetty, you needed to demonstrate Expert C2 level English to register. That ruled out most of my friends, who wrote English like gorillas. There were just six of us, four women and two boys, reading, or in some cases, looking mutely at translations of the great classic. And it's amazing how different that Shining Prince is when you read about him in different Englishes, different Frenchs, modern and classical Japanese. His poems, his clothes, his meals, his emotions are changed everywhere you look. You read thousands of pages, thousands of scrolls, thousands of screens, and still you never quite catch Prince Genji. You see him playing hide n' seek with all his lovers and their lovers, and you envy them because they can, however briefly, look him straight in the eye and smell his flesh, but you can't. Flipping through pages of the volumes at uneven speeds, the day escaped me. What I would have given to hear Genji's voice in my ear just once.

It was easy getting to White Cloud now that I knew what I was doing. I waltzed into the Small Studio, absurdly but cleanly dressed, exactly fifteen minutes before Kendo Forms started, as indicated on the schedule. I was a little nervous to see Iris again; I knew a warm welcome would not be forthcoming, but nervous is good. It means you're pushing yourself outside your comfort zone. I milled around by myself for a couple of minutes, inspecting the racks mounted on the wood panelled walls with my hands clasped behind my back, to show myself-- and Iris, if she suddenly appeared, that I wouldn't touch a weapon without permission. I figured she was going to be considerably late since we hadn't even crossed paths in the changing room. I had just released my left hand to dart out and rub a leaf of the bonsai tree when a voice behind me said, "It's fake." I jumped in fright and turned around at the same time, in a kind of panic ballet, to face Masahisa. How he looked in that instant stays with me, forever in ever refining detail, not at all like a memory, but like a hologram, still rendering and becoming sharper each time I turn it around. His long feet, planted solidly on the tatami, were clad in the midnight blue *tabi* Shizuka had wrapped in violet tissue for him. Brushing his insteps, the hem of his indigo-dyed *hakama*, the "pleated kimono skirt" of Mishima's translator. The knots across his hips were tight and even. His indigo-drenched top, an austere version of the fanciful kimonos I sell often, was crossed over up close to his throat, left over right, flattened against his waist. He emanated the night we were in together. Every stitch holding his uniform on his body was the same rich, blackened navy. I could've counted them all in an omniscient flash-- every pixel of him was sharp, revelatory against a dissolving background. Without his cap, he was older-- his thick hair wasn't the nylon black I'd imagined, but a striated silver. That detail shocked me, but didn't inhibit the sense that I was staring into my destiny. His face was stippled with the black stubble that gave him the look of a long, hard day behind him. His eyes burned in black nothingness. I stood frozen. It would be impossible to say he looked glad to see me. Without walking toward me, he said from where he was, "Class is cancelled today. It's on the web page."

"I--"

He interrupted me, still in his statue position near the door. "I don't know how serious this disease really is… anyway, no one else is coming… there aren't enough people to practice *kendo no kata* anyway…"

"Should I go?" I asked in a forlorn tone.

"Have we met?"

"Yes."

"Here? No, Iris said you came for the first time yesterday."

"I work at Boutique Shizuka."

"Right. Ok, there's hand sanitizer over there. Let's do a class." My heart was pounding and my stomach flipping. "Did Iris not give you a uniform yesterday?"

"No, I just wore this."

"Right. Because she thought you wouldn't return. Ok, forget it. Wear that for now." I courteously over cleaned my hands. "Sit on your feet two meters in front of me." I knew, this time, that meant facing him. "I intended to practice alone today. I'll teach you that. You're not qualified for that, but the situation is... different." He tossed a wide, tattered, white *obi* at me and told me step-by-step, without ever approaching, how to tie it on. Then he told me which sword, in a black sheath, to take off the wall. "Not that one. Third from the bottom." To my eyes, they all looked alike, but clearly the third from the bottom was the least precious. I went to great pains to avoid glancing at the mirrored wall. One doesn't easily forget the sight of a stout ballerina with a sword in her belt. I was impressed by his ability not to laugh; that as much as anything proved his fine character. Also his patience was remarkable. For the next hour, he demonstrated and corrected from a distance dozens of gestures whose names I couldn't memorize and whose purpose he didn't explain. I gamely followed along until I cut my hand on the tip of the steel blade.

"Really?" he asked with that note of incredulity, "but it's so blunt." He threw me a box of band-aids. "Wow," he added hurtfully. Still, bleeding from a wound I'd gotten in this unusual way, in close proximity to him, was something to cherish. I could scarcely believe how well I'd managed to find him, considering the vastness of the world. It was time for the boring part again, almost the same as yesterday's, but with extra steps for the different weapon. I nodded like a puppet as he went off on a riff about the mind is the sword... the sword is the mind... it's all emptiness, etc. I knew it couldn't be all emptiness because my heart was full of love. I replaced my practice sword on its rack.

"No." I thought I'd put it upside-down, but he said, "I have to teach you how to clean it."

"Oh." I brought it back.

"All your skin cells are on it. Do as I say." Well, that was my introduction to the imaginary sport called *iaido*. I hadn't retained much, but I got that I was cutting down adversaries in my mind, at whom I was supposed to be unflinchingly staring. He pulled out a wooden box, lifted the lid off with two hands, and took out a little stick with a bulbous top that belched white dust as he tapped his steel blade with it. I caught myself audibly mumbling, feeling like little Takeshi flopping around in his cage. "Excuse me?" he asked expectantly. Not waiting for my stammered reply, he volunteered, "Mine is cleaned differently from yours because mine is sharp."

"Sharp?"

"Yes, but yours is dull. Maybe one day you'll get a sharp one."

"I doubt it!"

"If you doubt it, then don't worry, you'll certainly never have it." I wanted to stand up and kiss him, so I looked down until he said, "Thank you very much," not to me, just generally, then to me, "Now you can put it back." I obeyed, studying the others before moving, to be sure I was facing it the same way. Instead of heading to the changing room, where he clearly wanted me to go, I drifted back to my spot two meters from him. He was still sitting, but had moved off the tops of his feet to a lop-sided lounging pose with one knee up, one down, like a house of cards, elbow on knee, chin on hand. He wore an expression of contented boredom. I looked down at my ridiculous get-up and saw that I still had on the borrowed belt. I unwound it. It dangled limp from my hand, trailing the mat. He held out his tanned hand. "Give it to me. Watch how I roll it." I tossed it like a bone to a dog and began to watch. "Sit down," he said, an exasperated sigh waiting on the periphery of his voice, but never quite coming in. I sat criss-cross apple sauce, the way Anglo kids said it on the playground. Masa's eyes were trained between his hands, where the *obi* was rolling up like cable wire, otherwise he would have seen my cellulite settle with gravity inside its pale pink casing.

"May I ask questions?" I asked too primly.

"Go ahead."

"What was this?"

"In what sense?"

"What was it called?"

"Which?"

"This that we did. It wasn't Kendo Kata. What was it?"

He smiled for the first time, a smile imbued with rays of the sun. "Oh! You mean which discipline? Oh my god. I never said. It's *iaido*, style *Muso Shinden Ryu*." I nodded, avoided repeating it. He smiled at me again, the transformative smile, limitless. "Sorry, I'm a terrible teacher."

"No, I--"

"I'm not the real teacher. I told you, I came to practice alone. Madame Mori explains better."

"Madame Mori?" I pictured a Japanese woman with a lined face and steel grey chignon.

"My wife. Iris-sensei. You met yesterday." It was as if postcards with pictures of them together on the front and jealous messages on the back were filling up my head in stacks. My job was to file them away. "Listen," he concluded with brusqueness, "We're closed until further notice. Just check the web page everyday. When we reopen, you can become a member and buy a uniform if you want. Send my regards to Shizuka."

I changed clothes as fast as possible, acutely, uncomfortably aware that, somewhere in the men's changing room, he was doing the same and would be waiting for me to leave so he could go home for supper. Sure enough, when I emerged, he was waiting just inside the threshold to the street. I shuddered to think what other things could be out there. My legs were reluctant to move. He was wearing a slight variation of his look, maybe just the non-rain version: today's baseball cap was in black velvet, with a black embroidery logo I couldn't discern, an unbranded grey heather hoodie with a steel zipper zipped up all the way up, indigo jersey infinity scarf, Adidas Y-3 track pants (a bit cliché, but hey) in white-on-black (yes, as I said, a bit cliché), and black neoprene ankle boots with a center zipper in thick, black plastic. I wondered where his bag was. I walked to him, stopping short of entering his personal space. "Why do you use a sharp one?" I dared to ask.

"Because it's real. Real is better than fake."

"You're not afraid of slicing yourself?"

"I am, but I'm very careful."

I can't imagine ever voluntarily playing around with a sharp blade. Even when I slice a baguette, I watch my fingers carefully and I would never do it for its own sake, only because I needed a piece of bread.

* * *

The bearded baldie shuffles around some blue folders, stands up and opens the window wider, thinks better of it and returns it to its narrow crack position, sits down again. He rubs his chin in a pantomime of cognition. "And this was your first conversation with Mr. Mori?"

"Second," I correct.

"The first being?"

"The first being," I mimic, "at my work-place."

"Yes, right. So, this was your first private conversation?" He writes something down, maybe a reminder to order cat litter, maybe a brilliant criminological insight.

"I suppose so."

"May I call you by your first name?"

"I don't see why not."

"Huguette, you said before that Mr. Mori, Masahisa--"

I cut in, "He's not here to grant you permission to use *his* first name."

"No. My apologies." He adjusts the folds of his turtleneck. "You said before that, during the course of this first private conversation, Mr. Mori told you, quote, 'The closer one is to death, the more pleasure one can feel.'" He pauses as though he's asked a question. I sit and examine my profoundly pink nails. They've held up remarkably well. "Huguette, do you still maintain that those were his words?"

"Yes."

"How did they strike you at the time?"

"How did what strike me at the time?"

"His words."

"I don't know."

"Did you find it bizarre? Unusual? That a stranger would say, 'The closer one is to death, the more pleasure one can feel.'?"

"Bizarre? Not really bizarre because it sounds like something people in the martial arts might say. I've never taken a class before. I dance."

The woman pipes up, "You thought he was showing off then? A little male peacocking?"

"Not really. He had a very low-key manner about him. And just going back to *your*--" I tilt my chin at her colleague-- "question, I was far from a complete stranger. I was a new student, on top of being an object of lust." All present exchange charged looks. "Object of lust" triggers doubt, embarrassment, amusement, concern.

The bald man says challengingly, "Mrs. Mori," he looks down at his notes, "Iris Mori tells us her husband had a strong preference for slim blondes, to the exclusion of all other types."

"And?" I can challenge too.

"And," he continues, while his partner struggles to keep her poker face, "it's implausible at best that Mr. Mori harbored an attraction to you."

I shrug, "What's impossible for you is probable for another man." His partner breaks down and passes him a scribbled note. He doesn't look at it, though; he looks straight into my opaque eyes.

"Ok," he breathes, "tell us again what prompted this dramatic statement."

I inhale deeply and let out, "I asked him if he ever found it disturbing to practice these beautiful movements with a deadly weapon. He said it didn't disturb him at all, on the contrary, the closer one is to death, the more pleasure one can feel. Then he said that he wasn't afraid of Coronavirus, as he walked toward me. I was afraid of the virus, but I thought the odds of him having been exposed to it were infinitesimal, so I didn't back away from him. I stood, feet planted on the checkerboard floor of the hallway. He came closer very slowly, not making a sound. It was like he was gliding on a track, floating on magnetic energy. As he got even closer, time slowed. I could feel his body heat intensifying with proximity. I could smell his *eau de cologne*, Mugler by Thierry Mugler, also getting stronger the further he ventured into my radius. He reached out a naked hand and stroked my loose hair, from the roots down to the split ends, over and over, with an even rhythm, without saying a word. He used such light pressure, it felt like a breeze stirring treetops. I'm short, but so was he. Our faces were exactly level. I could smell the anise drop dissolving on his tongue."

"Could you please slow down just a bit?" the interpreter implores me. The words are tumbling out of my mouth, a torrent stream of English.

"I was incredulous. I couldn't believe what was happening. I mean, how often in life is love, or even lust, reciprocated? I was right, goddammit, vindicated. It was a *coup de foudre* at the cash. There was a reason I came in to work on my day off. There was a reason he bought socks on that very day."

"The reason?" asks Baldie, stroking this time his own jacket cuff, as though evaluating my silent accusation of poor quality.

"Destiny is everything, I would say. It's the glue that holds together all the disparate elements of a life. It's the why in between every who, what, where, and when." That last stroke of philosophy makes me acutely aware suddenly of the video camera, tiny as it is, a dedicated phone really, on a bendy, little tripod with black and white legs perched on the table facing me. Its eye is as black and as flat and as cold as Masahisa's. I don't wait for permission to continue. I'm speaking to the eye more than to the police and the embassy staff. "The smell of anise commingled with Mugler cologne was uninterrupted by sweat. There must have been a shower in the men's locker room. I'd seen none in the women's. The scent molecules floating up my nose and into my mouth had an effect like a strange drug, soporific and stimulating at the same time. I felt like I could fall asleep, drop into his arms and into an exciting dream. But I forced myself alert. I wanted to memorize every single detail of this singular moment, to recall afterwards."

"After what?" the woman cuts in, breaking the flow of reminiscence.

"After it was over. You see, it all felt too good to be true, so I thought the moment would abruptly end, never to be repeated, so I wanted to be able to recall and relive it. Like I am now." She nods, a neutral nod that doesn't betray her opinion. I go on, "He brought his hand to my cheek, held it there. Energy was pouring out of his palm, soaking my face like a rainstorm. I saw surprise ricocheting around his features, like he didn't know what he was doing or why. In slow motion, he kissed me on the mouth, the lightest first kiss I've ever experienced, like the first touch of moss to grow on a forest rock. His fingertips caressed my neck with the same moss-like lightness. Then he stopped and stepped back. He asked me, 'Do you agree?' I nodded hard, shaking off the hesitancy of the first kiss and first caresses." Everyone at the table stares at me with a unanimous impression of my being batshit crazy. But I'm not; this is me in love. This is how I talk, in English, about love. At school, they called me a nerd and said I was trying to sound like a book. They said that when I mumbled to myself, I was rehearsing my nerd speeches. Today they can't be mean until they go off-duty.

"Huguette, after giving your consent for sexual contact, what happened next?"

I take a deep breath, hold it, and sigh. "He asked me if I had to work the next day. I said I didn't. He said his work was cancelled, too. He asked me to meet him here at fourteen hours the next day. I agreed and brushed past him to leave."

"And he stayed behind?"

"Yes, but it looked like he was on his way out, too."

"Did you see him leave?"

"No."

"You didn't turn around for one last look?"

"No, I was focused on safely getting home."

"He didn't offer you a lift or offer to accompany you to the station?"

"No."

"Did that bother you?"

"I didn't think about it."

"You didn't think of the previous night's assault?"

"I did think of that, so like I said, I concentrated on my surroundings, looking out for potential danger, or even for Pierre, to thank him, but no, I didn't think to myself about Masa taking me home."

"So you never saw him come out."

"No."

It's normal for me to not remember pivotal events. I have black holes in my memory for some of my life's most exciting moments. I remember being in the first day of kindergarten, looking down at my smocked calico pinafore hanging straight down my body, without knowing how I'd gotten there. I remember the applause and the whistles as I accepted the Japanese Language Medal, seeing my orange leather Camper mary-janes attached to the glossy wood, like a basketball court, of the auditorium stage, drawing a blank about leaving my seat, navigating the long aisle and stage stairs. I don't remember the trip home from the dojo that night. It must have been uneventful. I did forget to cover my face and hands against the virus. I know this because the next thing I remember is the perfume of rose petals wafting up into my face from a tea canister. I was standing in my kitchen, holding a tea scoop, still in my coat, my shoes neatly left at the door, the mask and gloves folded in my pockets where I'd left them. I put down the scoop to smell my hands. Sure enough, I'd already washed them. The smell of soap was strong and fresh, and they were still damp. My nails still were ten dewy petals, glossy at the end of each stubby finger. In my own home, I could talk out loud as much as I wanted to. It had begun to rain again, and the pitter-patter on the windowsill talked over me. My whole body was vibrating with eagerness to see him again. I called Yvonne, but it went into voice-mail without ringing. I paced around in circles, thinking things through. When would Shizuka re-open the shop? Or maybe she would drop dead from the contagion. I would need to make money very, very soon. A good night's sleep was essential. I got into bed, pulling the Seidensticker *Genji* under the camellia print duvet with me. I flipped to the *Lavender* chap-ter, where the Shining Prince grapples, to him-self and everyone else, with his erotic obses-sion with the little girl. He wants to adopt her, but the girl's nanny, Shōnagon with the lustrous black hair, is reluctant. Genji explains himself: "I have made my own feelings clear, over and over again. It is precisely the childlike quality that delights me most and makes me think I must have her for my own. You may think me complacent and self-satisfied for saying so, but I feel sure that we were joined in a former life."

When I woke up the next morning, I rubbed avocado oil into the tips of my hair and left it on for fifteen minutes. If he could come in on a Sunday just to see me, I could show up with healthy hair. The sky was blue; the sun was shining; the birds were chirping. The city itself spruced up for our *rendez-vous*, nature itself whistling a tune, happy to be our third wheel. Checking first for vacancy, I stepped into the empty hall in my pyjamas (this time the *toile de Jouy* in pink and white, the best), bronze Birkenstocks, my head turbaned in aqua terry. I gingerly rang Alain's doorbell, one quick push with low pressure, in case he was still asleep in the late morning. The door opened immediately, as though he'd had his hand on the doorknob when I rang, about to go out, or maybe disinfecting it with bleach. His cargo shorts and coffee bowl told me I'd just disturbed a relaxing morning. I apologized pro-fusely before he could say a word. He nodded and smiled until I finished, an apology coach.

"A pleasure, always a great pleasure to have a run-in with the Queen of the North. She emerges from her igloo palace in a thermal crown." He was cracking himself up. "How can I help?" He smoothed a red tee shirt down over his soft belly.

"Weird question, but do you have a pair of sweatpants I could borrow?"

He raised just one eyebrow; the other one was unfazed. "Sweatpants? Like training pants?"

"Yes. You see, I have a date to go running [it would be too complicated to get into the martial arts] and I don't have any track pants or anything and all the stores are closed. Double whammy: Sunday and viral outbreak."

"Are you sure it's wise to exercise now?"

"It's at a private gym."

"On treadmills?"

"Yes! Treadmill date."

"You know, you should leave one empty between you."

"Good idea."

"And don't kiss him afterwards."

I blushed. "No, of course not. It's a first date."

"A lucky fellow. I burn with jealousy, you know."

I could feel my face's flush becoming hideous. "I think we wear about the same pants size."

"Yeah, yup." His eyes darted sideways to avoid discussing my lack of waistline, and his expansion. "I have grey and I have blue, my dear."

"Is the blue a dark or a bright blue?"

"Bright, light, an azure."

"Then, the grey, please."

"Good choice, I'll be right back. I'd invite you in, but I haven't tidied up."

If only Masahisa had led me to a running track, I would've been spared a lot of hassle. Running has such a calming simplicity to it, right foot, left. Starving and stimulated to see him again, I was dreading the sports component. Butterflies played tag in my stomach as I anticipated our meeting.

The long train ride to the hate crime scene took on the flavor of a pilgrimage, familiar enough to inspire confidence, ritual enough to feel monumental. I'd suffered a lot on that spot, but had also felt the most stirring ecstasy of my life. Dreams do come true and mine did. Masa was on his way, at the same time, to see me. Of all women in the world, me. I hated the idea of pulling those unflattering pants over my thighs and appearing before him like that, but I knew that with him, unlike all other men, my looks didn't matter. It was our souls that were attracted like magnets, and you couldn't ruin a soul with a tight pair of pants.

Those evil pants did cling to me like a plague as I emerged from the decayed changing room. I processed up the corridor, fatefully navigating the checkerboard, red, black, red, black until I got to the amber glowing doorway of the Small Studio. I could hear his heart beating from within. I could smell the pheromones emanating off his skin. I could feel his anticipation of risk. We were a glowing red dot at the center of the map of the world; all around us, the world was prepping to distance themselves from each other; we were preparing ourselves for the physical union of our lives, the touch that would discipline pleasure and make it our slave.

I stepped onto the tatami, Alain's sweatpants chafing my inner thighs. Just then, the sad thought came to me that I should have fixed him up with Yvonne. Why had I never thought of that? Stupid me, she would have loved it. Masa was sitting on his feet with his sword at his side and a second one two meters

away. He appraised me with a vertical scan.
"Thanks for coming," he said curtly.

"Thanks for having me," was all I could think to say, although I instantly regretted it. It sounded like I was helping myself to a double slice of quiche at a brunch buffet.

"Today because there is nothing else to do, I'll teach you the nomenclature of the sword. This way, when the usual students come back, you'll know what they know. Ok?" I nodded, feeling very much the imposter. I didn't give a fig about the sword and wanted nothing less than to ever meet the usual students. I could already picture them: a ragtag cohort of Japanese porn loving machos. I recall at that moment regretting that Masa hadn't led me to an Irish step dancing club. He embarked on a set of explanations that would have been interminable if not issuing from his pure and graceful mouth. I challenge myself now to recall everything he had me repeat. I'm going to force the police to pay close attention in case any of it is relevant. Blowharding about his stuff makes me feel closer to him. I clear my throat.

"So, the real, sharp sword is the *katana*. The blunted practice weapon is the *iaito*." They don't scribble because the video is getting everything. They look and listen. "The sheath is the *saya*. The handguard is called the *tsuba*..." I like seeing their eyes glaze over. They try to hide it, but it's in a certain immobility of the neck and the set of the jaw. "... the handle, or *tsuka* is wood covered in *galuchat* stingray leather, held in place by the bronze studs called *menuki*, then wrapped in overlapping bands of cow leather. On to the blade..." A slight twitch in Baldie's eye tells me an interruption is on the horizon. I trudge on, "... crafted of tempered steel, the blade consists of a non-cutting edge, the *mune* and of course, the

better-known cutting edge, the *ha*, which cul-
minates in the *kissaki*--"

Every bit as predictable as I'd predicted,
he has to say something now. "You memorized
this all during the course of that one lesson?"

"In a way, well, no. I have a very good
word memory. So, I probably could have, but
as I told you before, I went straight from the
lesson to the Musée Guimet, where I rein-
forced what I'd learned in the galleries."

The woman says, "Let's not get there
yet. Let's stay on the details in this private lesson."

"Sure," I say in a fake obliging tone.
"Did I say yet the *bohi*? The blood groove?"

She insists, "You said before that at the
conclusion of this class, you and Mr. Mori con-
summated the implied agreement of the day
before and had sexual relations?"

I lick my lips, savoring what I'm about to say. "Yes. That's it. We never did any exercise or anything. We never stood up. It was more like a school lesson, but without taking notes. He had me repeat after him and told me that if I forgot anything, later I could look it up on the internet, where tons of diagrams and stuff could be found. I told him that I didn't really need to have worn activewear. Street clothes would have been fine for what we were doing. He snapped his fingers and said that reminded him that he could give me a uniform, if I had decided to join, because one must never, never train in not a uniform. He repeated 'never' like that: never, never. He said it wasn't a problem if I didn't have money at that moment. I could take the uniform home, wash it, make whatever alterations it would need, and have it ready for when the dojo reopened for classes. I could pay then."

My stomach tightens at the memory. I would never say this part out loud. Some things you keep inside you so they don't spill everywhere and make everything dirty. He said, without making eye contact, "They're uni-sex, so not so well proportioned. I'll give you a Large, but it'll be too long, so you can hem it at home."

"Could I try the Medium?"

"The Medium won't fit you," he said tersely. "Wait here." I sat fuming while he went to another room. He wasn't even going to let me *try* the Medium? It was that inconceivable? He was *confident*: the men's Large, made for an enormous, tall guy, would be just right? I felt the blood burning in my neck. Knowing it was verboten, I stood up and walked over to where his *katana* stood propped in a corner, away from the practice weapon racks, wrapped in a tube-like bag of what looked like raw den-im. I listened for his footsteps. Hearing none, I

144

untied the bag and let it slide down the gleaming black lacquer sheath. It still stood propped,
like an idol. I glanced over my shoulder at the
doorway leading out into the still empty, silent
hall. The red and black squares, which had
before looked greasy, now struck me as sinister, the board of a bad game. This floor had
been faded by mis-deeds and cover-ups. Of
their own will, my hands reached out and
stroked his sword, grabbing the grip that had
been broken in by millions of droplets of his
sweat. I picked it up. It was heavier than it
looked, heavier than the one I'd borrowed. The
sheath slid off it downwards, dragged by gravity, thumping the floor at my feet. I was left
holding a cold, exposed blade. I panicked, but
I didn't move a muscle; it was that paralysis
that comes with unanticipated danger. I was
holding my breath when I sensed him explod-
ing into the room, shouting, "No! That's not--"
It dropped out of my hands like a *guillotine*.
Time stopped. Masa's open mouth, his reach-

ing hands, a strand of hair stuck to my eyelid, the obscene emptiness between my hands, all should have been momentary sensations, but they solidified into monuments to my humiliation. When time restarted, it was hurtling down on a bias, away from my feet, but the sharp side grazed my thigh. I felt sensation where I shouldn't have, even fresh air, on a part of my flesh that was supposed to be covered in dappled grey, spongey cotton. Before it landed, it struck the tatami and blew it up like a grenade. It came to rest beside the trench it had torn. Blood dyed the rip in Alain's pants and was spreading outward. "*Merde*," hissed Masa. He sprinted over to me with a crimson face, the one Japanese men get when they've been drinking. He was drunk on disappointment. "*Merde*," he said a second time, louder, as though confirming a diagnosis. "Press it with your hands. I'll be back." I should have been horrified, but I was vacant. It was like the cut was bleeding out my thoughts. He raced back in, dishevelled not in physical aspect, but in mood. "Lie down on your back." I spread out on the tatami. Now he was all business, no profanity. He slid fabric under my tensed hands, over the wound, that I couldn't immediately identify. I half sat up to get a look at it: a cream colored *tenugui* with porcelain blue stripes and unfinished hems. The rough edges and fresh blood stains lent it a foreboding beauty, evidence of our connection. He must have thought I was worrying about the blood loss because he traced my gaze from thigh to eyes and said mildly, "Don't worry. It looks like a lot of blood, but it's superficial. You're lucky. No serious damage."

"Are you a doctor?" The child inside me posed the question like a ritual prayer.

"No. I'm a *coiffeur*, but I know what I see." He spoke while his hands moved. "We can't go to the Emergency Room."

"Why not?" I was still in juvenile mode.

"You want to contract the virus? I'm not taking you."

I lay back down and closed my eyes, trying to enjoy his busy hands on my leg. After some patting and rustling, I opened them again and noticed that the ceiling was painted a pale lemon. "All done," he said softly over the sound of rubbing sanitizer into his hands. I'd just opened my mouth to thank him, when he added, under his breath, "Imbecile."

"Can you repeat that?" My voice was shaky.

He ignored me. "It's just a deep scratch. I cleaned it and glued it closed. There's gauze taped over it. You'll need that to change the dressing, so if you don't have it at home, you'll need to stop at a pharmacy for some. Also, keep it clean."

"I'm not an imbecile." He blinked at me, saying nothing. "I made an innocent mistake." He was gathering up his things, packing up the First Aid kit that had been thrown into disarray around him. His jaw was clenched. He stood up with the red and white nylon case and walked to the doorway. Poised over the threshold, he stopped and said over his shoulder, "Do you need me to get you an uber?"

"I have my own account, but I don't like it much. Can we have a do-over? Tomorrow?"

"Seriously? Are you a madwoman?"

"No, I--"

"Please. Never set foot in here again." He turned his head and disappeared. I could hear his linoleum footfalls to the men's changing room and then the metallic rummaging in a locker. My haunch was throbbing, but not really hurting. There must have been a numbing agent in the antimicrobial he used. My gaze darted around the room, skipping between his personal effects still scattered around. It must have been rare to catch him in sloppiness. He'd been caught off-guard. A posh looking water bottle with a wood grain finish caught my eye. I grabbed it and hobbled into the women's room.

I'm rescued from my unpleasant memories by my lawyer prompting, "Huguette, you're being asked a question."

"Oh, sorry." I look around at the dispiriting *décor* of the interview room. A handwritten sign affixed to the wall with masking tape advises: WASH YOUR HANDS / DON'T TOUCH YOUR FACE.

She says, "Walk us through again what happens when he leaves the training floor to get you a uniform."

I sigh. They're tediously thorough. I'd hate to have her job, though I'd love her figure. "He went to the back or wherever, I don't know, to get me a uniform. While I was waiting, I walked over to where his sword was balanced upright in the corner."

"Why?"

"Just to have a better look. It was beautiful and I wanted to look at it. I took it out of its… carrying bag, I guess… I'd never held one before. I thought the blade was locked into the sheath, not locked, but… clicked into it, secured by a clasp. So, I didn't think it would slide off so easily. I was shocked when it did. I panicked and dropped it. It hit my leg. Luckily, it just grazed it, so I didn't get seriously injured."

Baldie throws in with a quizzical expression, "And your cane?"

"Totally temporary. I hardly need this cane. I use it only to take pressure off that leg when I walk. It's sore. That's it."

He nods. "So you use a cane for a scratch?"

"A cut." I smile. "If you watch a samurai movie, you'll understand better."

Stiff chuckles from across the table. I clear my throat. "At that point, Masahisa came rushing in. He raced to my side repeating over and over, chanting really, yes, he was chanting, like a mantra, 'No, no, no, my poor darling, my poor darling.' Were it not for the pain, I would've comforted *him*, he was so distraught. But cool, level headed. 'Wait here,' he said. He laid me down on my back, pressed my hands to the wound, and there he paused for a split second. His two hands on top of mine, our twenty fingers splayed over the blood like the petals of a flower growing on the bank of a flooding river, he looked into my eyes. His eyes were blacker than usual. His pupils were dilated and brimming with the ink of a dozen love letters. 'I love you, Huguette,' he whis-pered, like it was a secret that surprised even him. He pulled off over his head the steel grey cotton tee shirt he was wearing-- I couldn't tell if he'd had it on all along under his uniform or had changed into it-- and folded it under my head like a little pillow. He dashed away and I had a few seconds to look at the yellow painted ceiling and digest what he'd said to me. Of course, I felt the same way, but it was so sudden, so irrational, it blew me away that he felt it too. He rushed back in, still bare chested, holding a red and white First Aid kit. He sat on his feet beside my thigh and apologized for the pain he was about to cause me. The thing I remember most clearly, because it stood out, was him saying, 'We can't go to a hospital. The virus is there. Don't worry, I'm going to fix this myself. It was my fault this happened, but please don't worry. I've dealt with worse here many times.' He very gently removed my hands one by one from the cut, all the while murmuring 'It's ok, not too bad, not at all deep.' He wiped away the blood with the blue and white *tenugui* you have in evidence. Then he surprised me again.

He grabbed his S'well bottle, which I had assumed was filled with water, and dribbled the contents into my cut. 'It's chilled *sencha*,' he explained, 'It has antimicrobial properties. The samurai used to use it for this.' It felt so soothing. Later, when I had the chance to think about it, I was surprised that you could put tea in a S'well. I don't think you're supposed to, though I'm grateful he did, but at the time, I just admired his ingenuity under pressure. Then he dried it with a paper towel, the brown kind from the wall dispenser, and superglued it shut and covered it all with a white dressing, white gauze and white tape. I was still reclining on the tee shirt pillow. He cleaned his hands and lay down on the tatami next to me, his nose centimeters from mine. His amber shoulders shone with perspiration. Do I go on?"

"Please," says the woman, looking un-comfortable.

"It's just sex," I say. "A universal. Should I skip over this part?"

"Leave out the graphic details, but we have to go over again exactly what you talked about."

I clear my throat. I'm choking myself up. "He held my face in his hands and began kiss-ing my ear. It felt wonderful, like being nibbled by butterflies. Then he kissed my mouth with passion. He told me again that he loved me. He said he loved me more deeply than he'd ever loved anyone in his life. He loved me more than he loved life itself. He whispered fast, a deluge of phrases that gushed out of him like the blood from my gash. He said that karma had brought us together, unfinished des-tiny from another life. He said that the moment he'd laid eyes on me at the shop, he'd been drawn to me by an inexorable, undeniable force. He understood what he'd been looking for his whole life. He said he'd tried to create a pretext for getting to know me then, but because he's married and goes way back with Shizuka-- he implied they'd been lovers years before, and had remained friends, maybe even lovers too, he didn't say, throughout his marriage-- he couldn't go any further. He was gripping both of my hands so tight as he confessed to all this, it felt like he could break the bones in my hands. I didn't care. I felt the same. He kissed me again, full of emotion, frantically. He told me that when Iris had come home and described a new student, he didn't dare dream it was me because the odds were too low, so he came by himself the next day, and he was lucky that the Coronavirus had caused to be cancelled his Fashion Week gigs, that was karma too, and then he saw for himself the impossible-to-believe miracle that it was me, and he controlled himself, he disciplined his feelings into betraying nothing on his face, but he was as tormented as glad to meet his soul mate again.

Needless to say, at this point, I was wracked with terrible guilt for not telling the truth about having followed him, and letting him go on believing that it was all a cosmic coincidence, but I was ashamed. So ashamed. Of being a stalker, a trickster, an imposter. I was a liar, pure and simple, but his love was so honest, I couldn't ruin it. Could I? Then he was feverishly making love to me, on the floor. It was vigorous, but also he was so careful not to abrade my thigh, like only a man in love could be. I couldn't bring myself to come clean in the midst of this undeserved exquisite pleasure. He begged me, with tears in his eyes, after he came, to tell him if I felt the same, if I agreed that our lives were intertwined, that we had unfinished business from a previous life. I said yes, I felt the same. He asked me, clutching my head to his chest, if I'd follow him from this life to the next. I had no idea what he meant-- I took it as a metaphor-- so I said yes. He made me promise to meet him the next day at noon, in the Big Studio, the room next door. Of course, I thought he meant it as a … tryst, so I readily agreed, and right away started thinking about which underwear and bra I would wear. I knew he loved me for my soul, and that superficial impressions weren't important to him, but still I wanted to be pretty for him, as one always wants to be pretty for a flesh and blood man, no matter how deep. I assured him I'd be there. We got dressed in a cloud of happiness. It all felt unreal, like floating through a dream. He was very solicitous about the leg, offering me his pants, offering to accompany me home, but I declined everything. I wanted to part on this euphoric high note. It would have been anticlimactic to go through the banality of seeing if his pants fit (besides, my coat covered the worst of it) or the banality of plugging my address into a map, getting stuck in traffic, talking about high rents, blah blah blah. I had to assure and reassure him that I'd be fine getting myself home. He went over how I should re-dress the wound, then he kissed me goodbye and let me go.

And I really did intend to go straight home. I suppose, in retrospect, that the endorphins in my bloodstream were acting as painkillers-- and he had given me something from the First Aid kit, don't know if it was ibuprofen or acetaminophen or what-- but I didn't feel like resting. I'd just had the best sex of my life and was seeing the world with new eyes, as one does. I was so moved, I suppose, by the ambiance, the bonsai, the shrine, the tatami mats, I didn't think it consciously at the time, but that must be why, on a whim, I decided to go to the Musée Guimet instead of going home. It was like I wanted to extend my waking dream by walking amongst the Japanese art collection. In my daze, I'd forgotten

completely about the virus and despite knowing full well that the guards at the Louvre were
on strike, and rightly so, I didn't even think to
check if the Guimet was open. I just made my
way there-- it was far-- in a trance. They were
open. I was moving pretty slowly, with a limp,
and feeling drained at the same time as ecstat-
ic, so by the time I got to the entrance gate, it
was half an hour til closing. The woman at the
ticket desk, in glasses, chunky earrings, and a
hill tribe looking scarf, just as you'd expect,
asked me if I really wanted to spend my money
on a ticket, it was so close to closing, and she
wasn't allowed to wave me through. Wouldn't
it be better to come back another day? I in-
sisted. After all, I had no desire to go through
the whole museum. I've always loved the
Khmer gallery, but I've seen it more than once.
I only wanted a quick glance at the *tsuba*s.
She apologetically refused to take cash-- she

wasn't touching money-- so I used my debit card.

Half an hour in and out was sufficient. The *tsuba*s were really sublime. There weren't many on display, but what they had were in a double sided glass case, so you could examine both sides and appreciate the iconography so expertly rendered in metal. I went home a satisfied woman. It was probably the most complete, most gratifying day of my life. I remember thinking that I had lived my entire life all so that I could eventually live that day. I taped the postcard of a woodblock print I bought in the giftshop on my way out up on the front of the cabinet where I store the tea canisters."

* * *

"I would very much prefer never to see you again," was what Masa had said when I asked if I could come back the next day for him to inspect my wound.

I sniveled like a bratty toddler. "If hospitals transmit Corona today, they also will tomorrow. And clinics. And pharmacies. How do you expect me to get medical care?"

"I can't say I know." He looked away from me coldly.

"If it got infected and I lost my leg, I'd hate to see you held responsible." He faced me again, this time with a look of disgust mixed with rage.

"You're a madwoman. I've never met someone so selfish in my life. Now you're threatening me. I see. Good. Very well, come back here tomorrow. I'll look at it again. And

I'll give you better dressing supplies that I keep at home. And then we'll never cross paths again. Are we agreed?"

I wiped away dripping snot with the back of my hand. "What time?"

"How's noon?"

"Noon is perfect." A little smile lit up my puffy face.

"Please see yourself out, Madame," were his last, stiff words before disappearing into the men's room.

I limped to the station. My whole leg, not just the cut, hurt like a demon. My bag felt heavy. I was exhausted, but too wired to rest. I wasn't about to lock myself up in my flat like a caged animal. It's all mental, I told myself, reality is all mental. There's a positive side to every situation. While I attempted the Metro circus act of inching away from other passengers without touching a pole, I succeeded in finding the good in this. Look, people get scars for all different reasons, usually something depressing like surgery or acne. But an accident with a samurai sword? How unique was that? *C'est chic!* When it was all healed up, I wouldn't hide it. Oh no. *Au contraire.* I'd display it in a short skirt. I'd emphasize it. Yes, the way some women emphasize their slim ankles. It would enhance my sex appeal. Yes, perhaps I'd get a tattoo, not to conceal it, but to highlight it. Yes! A classical Japanese motif, a lush peony maybe, or Prince Genji's family crest. It was all a blessing in disguise. Impulsively, I decided to go straight to the Musée Guimet to research designs. My leg and head throbbed, and my pants were trashed, but who cares? It would redeem a shitty day.

The museum was open, but had a hollowed out mood. It was almost closing time and the staff looked like they'd seen enough faces for a lifetime and were ready to go on strike. I made a beeline for the *tsuba*s, which I'd glanced at before, but hadn't paid much attention. This time, I projected into the glass case, pressing myself against the cool metal, trying out their designs on my future scar. Floral, geometric, mythical-- the possibilities were endless. I snapped out of it and went to the Noh masks, a surefire stimulus to profound thought. The metaphors for life and love made themselves. I drifted over to some kimono textiles, my favorite. If you traced all the way back, it was antique kimono textiles that had brought me together with Masahisa. I'd always loved them. I'd given an oral presentation about them in Advanced-Intermediate Japanese. An A minus. Then when I first got here, I was strolling the Marais when I wandered into Boutique Shizuka. It had been empty, so I'd gotten to chatting with Shizuka. She was impressed with my language skills and she loved my hair. She offered me a part time job, which I accepted, thinking it temporary and way beneath me. Time passed and Shizuka moved on from wanting to run the shop all day, my position became full time, and I stayed. These gorgeous fabrics became my prison. They wrecked the skin on my leg. It was burning and aching. I felt lightheaded. I regretted the side trip. How much nicer it would be, more self-caring, to be home in my *yukata*, *obi* knotted loosely, so I can eat as much as I want. A bath would be amazing, but I probably shouldn't get it wet yet.

I wondered what *chez* Mori was like. Did Masahisa and Iris live in squalor near the dojo? Or at an elegant address closer to the salon? Or maybe in Neuilly? Had one of them family money? Or both of them? I wished I could be a fly on the wall in their bedroom… no doubt they wore cotton *yukata* at home, with striped sashes, the classic. That was a given. The only question was whether they were matching or inverse. I would say inverse, he in navy on white, she in white on navy. Only the *obi*s matched. Possibly the socks too. I re-called that he'd bought pairs of *tabi* in indigo and white, and possibly black. Those could have been for both of them; that would have explained the huge sock order. Either they co-ordinated with matching navy or white or went for the inverse, her in the blue with him in the white. Yuki's color chart came to mind, with its dazzling tolerance for variation. Poor Yuki and her broken heart, to be compelled to live alone in a narrow room like that, all because of some skirt-chasing mama's boy. The white spectrum would stun even First Nations ice dwellers in their seal mittens: Custard, Chalk, Cloud, fun-ny I could only think of ones with concise names. It nagged at me that I couldn't recall the longer ones, oh yes, like Pink Diamond, a rosy white with only the very faintest tinge, like the snow that falls over a rouge factory. Whenever I was looking at the wall chart and my eyes would alight on that one, I'd be reminded of that gargantuan pink diamond ring the heroine gets in the film adaptation of *Lust, Caution*, the stone that sets her on her inexorable course toward betrayal and execution, that's like a crystallization of her adulterous orgasms with the dapper war criminal. In the book, its color isn't specified. Eileen Chang was too masterful to tell us that. She plants a pink diamond in our minds only in a shred of gossip about some Shanghainese Marie Antoinette.

I had a strong feeling the Mori bedroom had pale pink walls, an iced carnation. No doubt they slept on twin futons, made up in pristine white linens, side by side. Sometimes their lovemaking would start on one, sometimes the other, often ending in the opposite one, or completely off it, on the bare parquet. They had herringbone floors, too beautiful to cover with carpet or tatami. They wouldn't even undress. That would waste time. Their bodies would join in a writhing mass of fabric

(iris print would be an obvious choice, otherwise pine branches for the forest of Mori), un-
dulating with gasping bliss.

A chime sounded for closing time. I
shuffled into the gift shop and bought a postcard. The sun had crumbled into the Seine by
the time I reached home. I hate nightfall in this
city. They only light certain *façades*-- they
never light mine. The pain had intensified. I
rammed six prescription strength ibuprofen
pills, left over from an oral surgery, into my
parched mouth and swallowed them in one
gulp of fridge water. I taped up the postcard. I
gingerly peeled off my clothes. The pants
looked like they'd been in a shark attack. I
couldn't return them to Alain like that. I'd have
to buy him a new pair, but I didn't know where
such pants were sold. I'd have to ask him. I
put up water for tea. I felt like a pot of genmaicha, Masahisa's favorite. That would be
soothing and anti-inflammatory, a good substi-

169

tute for the dinner I hadn't the heart to prepare. I grabbed an open bag of jam cookies from the cupboard. These would do. I desperately needed a shower, but didn't dare. I couldn't bear to disturb the inflamed mess under the bandage. Instead, I rubbed soap into my stinking, stubbly armpits and splashed them with cupped hands of running water from the kitchen tap.

I'm not an imbecile. He was probably telling his spindly wife that I was one, right then. The woman was no more than a wire frame carrying case for a set of hair extensions. His water bottle lay swaddled in my bag like a sleeping baby. His skin cells and respiratory droplets still coated it. Instead of wiping it down as recommended, I rubbed it against my cheek. There. Now it was as though he'd gently stroked my face, telling me not to worry about my little *faux pas*. All would be rectified. The smell of toasted rice, spongy and warm, filled my nostrils. The perfume of genmaicha is so earthy, so homey, your chum's friendly grandma is serving you afternoon tea while the bread for tonight's supper finishes up in the oven. I sloshed the straw hued liquid into a chipped Churchill Blue Willow teacup that used to be my own grandmother's, my real grandmother, who never baked bread. It rattled in its saucer as if even it were afraid of what I might do. I jammed a couple of cookies into my mouth, scattering crumbs across my bosom, washed it all down with a swig. It felt good going down. Caffeine plus sugar plus flour makes an empowering drug. No wonder Masa likes this tea so much-- it puts hair on your chest, as my grandmother used to say about her whiskey. I rolled his bottle up and down my cheek while I munched. I refilled my cup and let the steam waft into my face like a spa treatment before I drank any more. I was feeling much, much better. I set up a second pot. It steeped, over steeped actually: a second pass at genmaicha shouldn't exceed thirty seconds, but I had a good reason to pursue strong flavour. Under the kitchen sink, I keep a lime green plastic bucket filled with cleaning supplies. I pulled that out. A lot of the stuff was non-toxic, distilled white vinegar, tea tree essential oil, Yvonne's health nut folk remedies, but I had in mind something to kill germs with devastating finality. Outside, a wet pitter-patter started up again. No one even knew for sure how tenacious these Coronavirus particles were. What did it take to kill them dead? Somehow I doubted organic apple cider vinegar would do the trick. Bleach would. Disgusting, toxic, cheap, garden variety bleach kills indiscriminately, thoroughly, the angel of death that decimates fabrics even massively diluted, used in hospitals and morgues for peace of mind. I poured some into the wood-look bottle and swished it around. I knew that I had to spill it out and painstakingly rinse it, but I was feeling out of sorts.

I swished it around some more, with the elliptical gesture of a finicky wine taster. I unscrewed the black lid of the glass jam jar I use to store loose Canderel and I heaped spoon after spoon into his bottle. "Low glycemic index," I declared to myself in a can-do voice. I poured in the next layer, the second pot of toasted rice green tea. Second pots are always an interesting opportunity because the second brew contains significantly less caffeine than the first, with just as many life-saving polyphenols, and with an altered but in no way inferior taste. In fact, certain strains demand the first brew be dumped (or poured for servants and children), only the second or even third considered ideal for consumption. I breathed deeply over the bottle's mouth and recoiled. The bleach note certainly dominated the sencha note-- it was akin to having spilled a cup into a swimming pool (*piscine*, maybe my favorite word in the French language: pee-seen, the syllables force a muscular smile, sending signals to the brain of true contentment). I poured about a third of it down the kitchen sink, happily clearing the drain while I was at it. It reminded me that I was overdue to do something about the tangled copper bird's nest blocking the shower drain. I added more tea to balance the elixir. Then I popped it into the fridge door shelf, with the cap off so it would get cool. If you seal off a thermal bottle in the fridge, it stays lukewarm. When I first learned the word "lukewarm", I'd found it very strange. Luke? Why luke? And there's no "lukecool", though that would be a beautiful word, conjuring a liquid blue-green. *He had eyes of a limpid, lukecool aquamarine.* That would be a sensitive man, so different from a callous brute with cold blue eyes. I dumped in another heap of Canderel before slamming the fridge door.

I awoke on the kitchen floor to birdsong in the morning light. It was still early. My thigh pulsated. I streamed the news. This Corona nightmare was depressing. I got some classic *macha-iri sencha* going and brushed my hair. Thick orange wires pulled out and stuck in the brush. The powdered leaves gave off a primordial smell as they dissolved, the mist rising out of a purification ceremony. I drank it as much with my nostrils as my mouth.

I stood in front of my closet in my underwear and gauze bandage, looking in deliberatively, how one does before an occasion. It was imperative to be *chic*. I had to get dressed like someone smart and self-possessed, someone who didn't care about clothes, but who radiated poise. Someone with excellent hand-eye coordination and a casual familiarity with the classics. The rhomboid of sky visible from where I stood glowered grey. Paris was in a bad mood. I took the easy way out; I would lean on my trusty trick: you break every commonplace rule to rise above the ordinary. You don't specifically need magnificent hair for it to work, but you do need one stand-out feature.

Here it goes. I pulled out my navy pleated skirt. They say you should be skinny to wear pleats, but actually they're much better over flared hips than a straight line. Then a pair of black, ribbed tights. They say not to wear black next to navy, but that's like saying the night sky shouldn't share the horizon with the sea. Nonsense. Then of course my real Akoya pearls, purloined yet pure. Then my cream camisole, with a wedge of scalloped lace at the neckline, under a lightweight silk blouse in a milky shade of the pink they say redheads have to avoid like a plague, to echo the deep pink plague of my nails. I drummed my fingers against my chin, trying to imagine outerwear. I have a lipstick red merino trapeze coat that's a slap on the world's face on a chilly spring day, but that would be tipping my hand too much. No, restraint would be better. The charcoal cashmere blend with bracelet length sleeves, for a band of pink, collarless for pearl display.

* * *

"Monday morning," I'm telling the police, "I woke up in my bed, filled with anticipation. I couldn't wait to see him. It was literally the best day of my life and it hadn't even begun. I brewed my happy tea, Earl Grey. Bergamot is such a cheerful, hopeful smell. I choose my teas to reflect my moods, not change them, you see. For me, tea is an art, an expression, not a drug. I was walking on air. Cloud nine, as they say. I wore happy things, too. Pink is such a thrilling color and then my pearls. Those were the bridesmaid gift from my sister's wedding-- a beautiful memory-- and highly symbolic-- and appropriate. I thought there was a good chance Masahisa was going to propose to me."

The detective taps one of her pearl studs and cuts in, "Even though he was already married?"

I smile. "It's very hard to articulate a *coup de foudre*, but divorces happen all the time, everyday in fact, while meeting a soul mate is a once-in-a-lifetime experience." I bulldoze on ahead. "I passed the morning and the train ride as in a dream. The light inside White Cloud was different. I'd never been there at midday before. Natural light spilled in from unexpected angles. Maybe there were skylights I couldn't see. Some trick of the light gave Masahisa a halo where he was sitting on his feet, back to the shrine. He'd been waiting for me like that. 'Hello, Huguette.' His gaze made me feel pulchritudinous, a word I'd won an English spelling bee with in Sec 1. There was a benevolence in his eyes, a seeing-through, that told me he saw past my flesh, burrowing into my interior. His vision then concentrated, reversed, and came back out again, finding me beautiful and broadcasting it out. A ricocheting bullet. An eviscerating tender glance. The noontime light bleached his irises to a chestnut bronze I'd also not seen before. He and the dojo were one, changing together in the hours and the seasons."

* * *

Nothing kills a Grace-Kelly-on-the-Avenue-Foch look faster and more completely than rubber gloves and a disposable mask with a look of terror in the eyes above it. I could feel the sweat tie-dying the pink silk in my armpits as I rode the Metro, viral paranoia prompting me to shift on my feet every minute. All the riders were doing the same, all of us wishing at once we lived in the country. I got to White Cloud in a cloud of pain. My thigh took up about eighty percent of my proprioception. I believe that is the word for one's sense of orienting in space, one of the rare words I know in English only. It was like only my painful cut was real-- the rest of my body was a hologram. Masahisa was waiting for me on a backless wooden bench in the corridor. Cold fluorescent light bathed him in a rough, calloused glow. His face was strained. When I greeted him, he didn't even reply, just looked disappointed, as if even the way I say hello confirmed his low opinion of me. He gestured for me to follow him into the large studio. Our footfalls on the faded black and red checkerboard (more of a charcoal and dark pink, as you looked at them) were out of sync. His were regular; I limped.

"The light's better in here," he mumbled. He was in head-to-toe raw denim: selvedge jeans, an indigo overwashed lapelled jacket, and a pale chambray shirt. He was wearing another pair of our split-toe socks! Again, I saw them out of their Shizuka violet paper and on his feet. He'd worn them under black oiled leather Birkenstocks-- another thing we had in common-- which he'd stepped out of at the front door and left neatly, turned pointing out, away from me, the way a worshipper faces his rug to Mecca. The only touch of color any-where on him was a raw silk rectangular scarf loosely tossed about his neck. It was in a deep, mineral rust, with a minimal bronze thread running through it almost imperceptibly. It had unfinished edges, offsetting its luxury with an unpretentious provisionality. "It would have been easier if you'd worn pants," he intoned sullenly as he settled himself on the bare floor, opening the First Aid kit. I sheepishly shimmied my tights down over my hips and kept rolling until the crotch was at my knees. "Could you please remove entirely the hurt leg?" He asked this in a grumpy tone, while handing me a travel size bottle of hand sanitizer. The ribs of the tights had left deep vertical grooves in my flesh. The one uncovered foot and leg were pinstriped. He hummed to himself, a song I didn't know, as he pulled off the old dressing, whose interior was crusted about the same shade as his scarf. I was alarmed, but his face was impassive. No Alain-like compliments on my red toenails from Masa. He changed it all up without narrating anything, without reacting when I said "ouch", without looking at my face. As I was rolling my tights back up, he took something out of his bag I couldn't immediately recognize. At first glance, it was grey metal rods connected by sickly-looking plastic, tapering into a curve. For a split second, I thought it could be a suicide vest, but even in my agitated state, I couldn't buy the idea of Masa as jihad master. He set it down next to me. "Here. Take this cane. Keep it. I don't need it back."

"A cane?"

"It unfolds. You hold it on your good side to keep weight off your leg while it's mending."

"But it's so nice. I'll bring it back."

"No. Keep it. For me, it's bad luck. I don't intend to use it."

"What about when you're old?"

"I plan to die without a steep decline. Never stop training."

I fumbled, unfolding it into its cane shape. "Oh, thank you," I said, feeling foolish. I'd just thanked him for giving me his bad luck talisman of obviously depressing provenance. This had last belonged to someone who hadn't trained enough.

It was my turn to reach into my bag. I set up a little picnic on the gymnasium floor: two thick, squat Duralex glasses, a red and white gingham napkin laid out flat, on top of it, a scattered handful of cellophane wrapped fruit jellies, their flavours identified in Japanese script, that Shizuka had given me the previous Christmas. His face finally betrayed some-thing, somewhere between surprise and an-noyance. Before he could say anything, I said, "Since this is the last time we'll see each other, and I caused you so much trouble in such a short time, please, it's important to me, please, have tea with me. Let me thank you, just a tiny bit, not enough, let me apologize." He flinched, but said okay. I unscrewed the bottle.

"Is that mine?" His voice was incredulous. "What are you doing with that?"

"Sorry. Again, sorry about everything. I borrowed it yesterday for this. I made you genmaicha. Chilled, not iced, so it doesn't get diluted."

Without losing the shock in his voice-- this is the truest part of the story-- he said, "How did you know I love genmaicha?" I poured out two full glasses. I gestured to the sweets. "Please, help yourself. It would mean a lot to me." He took one at random and unwrapped it. I had pictured him as a nibbler, but I was wrong. He shoved the whole thing into his mouth at once and swallowed it after a minimum of chewing. I took my time reading each wrapper, settling on tangerine. I slowly removed its noisy wrapper, smoothed it out next to me on the ground, and ventured a hamster-like nibble. I raised my glass to my lips without drinking, just smacking my lips to make a sound and licking them to make them moist. It still smelled strange, but a night in the fridge had taken the chemical edge off. Without a first sample, Masa tilted his head back in a showily virile way and drained half the glass in one gulp. His mouth had contorted itself into a sneer by the time he lowered the glass. "Is this genmaicha?" I heard suspicion.

"Is it over sweetened?" I pouted, and an authentic tear dripped from one eye. I swiped at it with a knuckle. "I'm so embarrassed. I can't do one thing correctly."

"For god sakes, please don't cry. That's too much. It is way too sweet, but it's delicious," he lied like a gentleman. He drained his glass and set it down, grimacing. I wonder if he noticed that mine was still full? The pain seemed to overtake him instantly. It was so abrupt, like a digital effect.

"Excuse me," I said politely to his writhing form, as I stood up and stepped into the hall to empty my glass into the water fountain. When I limped back in (my thigh was newly sore from being handled), he was clawing at his throat, wide eyed, flopping around on the laminated wood floor like a goldfish spilled out of its bowl. Words escaped him.

From two meters away, I watched and waited patiently while he stopped flopping. When he was still, he was beautiful. So beautiful, it took my breath away. His face looked feverish and animated, livelier than when he was caring for me. I extracted my phone from my good purse. The lock screen was (I've changed it since) a snap of a postcard I bought my first time at the Louvre. It struck me and I liked it because it didn't show any art, at least nothing from inside. It's a photo of the museum courtyard at night, when the art is locked away behind layers of security measures.

There isn't a person to be seen; their absence beams brutal waves of silence out of the illuminated glass pyramid. Beyond, the city reposes in pools of light, glimmering reflections in darkness, beckoning and untouchable as a jewel display on black velvet, behind glass, inside another invisible security perimeter. "You're the one I came here for," I murmured to myself, fully conscious of it. I tapped one-five, fifteen being their 911. I started to cry and waited for them to come.

* * *

Inspector Baldie asks pointedly, "So when you arrived, Mr. Mori was in the small studio? Praying to the shrine?"

"I really couldn't say if he was praying. Maybe he was just sitting in front of it. I really don't know."

"Take us through-- again-- step-by-step what happened after you joined him in the small studio."

I clear my throat. I look around and take a deep breath. "'Hello, Huguette,' he said."

'You wanted to see me again?' I asked, really just out of nerves, obviously he wanted to see me. 'Let's move to the large studio,' he said. I didn't know why. I was kind of disap-pointed because the small studio is so much nicer. The big one is kind of like a gym without equipment. I figured he had his reasons, maybe something sexual. I didn't know.

He sat down. There's no shrine in that room, so I don't know how he chose his spot. I sat down two meters in front of him. He said, 'Come closer.' I crawled to him. Not sure why I didn't stand up and walk. It was like, maybe, not wanting to lose eye contact, or not wanting to raise my head above his. He didn't tell me to crawl. It's just what I did. When I got to him, he pulled me into his lap. His skin was hot, burning. His breath was spicy and clean, I re-member thinking he must have brushed and rinsed with some combination of cinnamon and baking soda. It wasn't minty. Or maybe he vaped that flavor, but I'm thinking that only now, not at the time.

He kissed me and ran his fingers through my hair. We made love." I blush. "You don't need details about that, do you?"

The policewoman's eyes dart left and right before she says, "It was consensual?"

"As I said before, absolutely consensual. The best of my life." Her eyes dart again, like she's reading a script.

"Go on, please, Huguette."

"The large studio is drafty. It was chilly, even in spring, so we both got dressed again. He held me in his arms and asked after my thigh. I lied and said it was fine and needed no further attention. I didn't want to block the flow of the moment, and anyway, the endorphins in my bloodstream were killing the pain.

He held me to him, so hard, almost crushing me. His arms were squeezing my ribcage. I'd never been so happy in my life. He whispered in my ear, '*Aishiteru.*' That's I love you in Japanese. '*Je t'aime.*' I told him I loved him too.

'Forever?' he asked me.

'Forever,' I assured him. I meant it. I knew he was the man of my life.

He grabbed both my wrists, tightly. His hands were like hot meat handcuffs. [I can't help giggling at "hot meat handcuffs".] [But I know one doesn't laugh in a police station. It makes one look crazy.]

'We're going to die together,' he said, pulling me, by the wrists, so close that the tips of our noses were close to touching. The channel of air between them was flowing up and down with hot and cold currents. If our noses did touch, sparks would fly.

'What?'

'I want us to die together, Huguette.'

'Die?' Because, you see, his French was accented, and you know how the Japanese blend the L and the R? *Mourir* could maybe have been something else-- what, I don't know, but-- it was so out-of-the-blue, apropos-of-nothing, that I had him repeat it several times.

'We will die together, Huguette.'

'Why?'

'Because it's correct.'

'It is?'

This part I don't remember verbatim:

I wish I could, though. It was so over-the-top: He said that he'd fallen in love at first sight with me at the boutique. He was a married man, an honourable man. He was not an adulterer. He said that he was convinced we'd been together in a previous life and that it had ended badly then, too. He said the Coronavirus was an enormous reckoning of the bad deeds of an entire society, that it would wipe out a lot of people in a wave of suffering, that most deserved it, but not all, a lot of innocent people would suffer and die too, it would be a *tableau* of misery, and that he wanted us two, if only just the pair of us two fate-bound, thwarted lovers to die healthy, uninfected, in each other's arms, untouched by the taint of disease or sin. He'd said we'd be together in a rare state of purity and would be reborn in a better position. In the next life, we'd be husband and wife, with nothing to regret, no retribution to fear, only a providential love to fulfill."

"But that's just a paraphrase?' she asks and states.

"Pretty much. I'm sure I've left something out. It was pretty baroque."

"What was your reaction to all that?"

"My reaction was shock. I've never been so stunned in my life and likely never will be again. I agreed with him one hundred percent about being soul mates. For sure when we met at the shop, it was a reunion of long-separated lovers, no doubt. But death? No way. I was thinking we should rent an apartment together, get a pet. I could bring him tea on a tray in the morning in bed. I tried to tell him no, but he kept repeating yes, yes, like a robot and he looked as if he couldn't even see me anymore, like he was alone, talking to himself. Yes, yes. Yes, yes. I was petrified. I had no idea what to expect. Was he going to take out a gun and shoot me? Lob my head off with a sword? My mind went blank. So when he pulled a water bottle out of his bag and set it on the floor between us, I was relieved. There was something normal. He was thirsty and overwrought, maybe even dehydrated, and could come to his senses. He unscrewed the top, took a long swig, then put it back down on the floor between us.

'Now you,' he said.

I asked him what it was. He said it was chilled genmaicha.

'No, thank you,' I told him. 'I don't really drink genmaicha. It's a men's tea.'

'Don't tell me you care about that bull-shit. We're in France.'

I relented and brought the bottle to my lips, but hesitated. 'It smells funny.'

He grabbed it out of my hands, took another long swig, and said, 'Look, it's sweet and delicious. You're just not used to my style.'

'What's in it?' I demanded.

'Like I said, genmaicha, my style.'

'And what else?' I was crying.

'And a ton of Canderel. And something to make us sleep together forever.'

When I heard that, I whispered, 'no, no, no' over and over and I grabbed the bottle and jumped up and emptied it into the water fountain in the hall. When I ran back, that was when he started-- he started--" I break down weeping, snot running, tears flooding. I'm gripping my own throat, clawing at it. I know my face is blotchy, redder than my mane. "I couldn't find my phone! I went digging around for it and it turned out to be in the same pocket where I always keep it, but I was like blind, my fingers numb. I was too panicked to see and feel. I dialled fifteen and sat and watched him die. I don't remember what I said to them, but I guess you have a recording of the call and the EMT's told you about everything."

* * *

After endless rounds of interviews, the detectives file out of the room, taking my lawyer with them. The interpreter drifts out by herself. I'm alone at the table with the pump bottle of hand sanitizer and extinguished tripod setup. It feels like a moment of manufactured reflection. I guess they're trying to make me think clearly, sort it all out. I tap my fingers against the tabletop. I wonder what color I should get next. Yuki will know. But if they prohibit spa services, I'll have to do my own nails for a while. Maybe I could see her just once more, for her to remove the pink, but just leave them unvarnished until the virus is over? I wonder if she does her own roots or goes out for them? I hope she does them herself. Staying home is going to be traumatic for bottle blondes. If Masa were still alive, Iris would be so lucky to be confined with a *coiffeur*. What will happen to her lips at home? I guess they'll deflate like party balloons. And her wrinkles will drain of fillers and reveal themselves. He'll never have any wrinkles. He'll never have to worry about the virus. And I'll never have to give him his cane back. It'll be my best souvenir of Paris, better than a postcard, better than a keychain of a mini Eiffel Tower. His skin cells are all over that cane, the way mine got all over that fake sword and had to be wiped off. His hands were all over it. I see his bronze hands deftly touching up her roots, pulling the pigment out to leave a crown of platinum on her head. I see them unwrapping each other like polite gifts.

My lawyer comes in alone, speaking to me in English. "Huguette, I have very good news. You're free to go. In recognition of the trauma you've endured, they're only going to ask for sessions with a social worker and a psychiatrist for an indefinite period. Thanks to the Covid threat, you're even going to do them from home, on your computer."

"Why is that very good news? I don't need a psychiatrist."

"Well, Huguette, I'm on your side. It's not for me to question your version of events, but as you know, the police don't believe for one second your version, your love suicide story. Under normal circumstances, they'd charge you with something-- obstruction of an investigation, filing a false report, misleading authorities, causing distress to the family, lots of Napoleonic Code stuff, but-- and I worked hard for this, please acknowledge-- given their strained resources with the shutdowns and your probable post-traumatic stress from the assault, not to mention witnessing a suicide, the recent loss of your best friend, the loss of your job-- Huguette, you've suffered a lot of strain, very much in the wrong time and place-- they're not treating your misreporting as a crime, just as a mental strain. This is a good deal. You're extremely lucky."

"But it was. It was a love suicide gone awry." I've always loved the word "awry". And "ajar". The kind of tricky adjective you'd never find in French. Our adjectives make sense. "We were in love. Passionately."

"Huguette, they've assigned Dr. ___, a wonderful, highly regarded practitioner who will lend an ear and help you sort out fact from fantasy. For right now, let's get you home."

"But I'm guilty."

"You're not guilty of anything."

"I feel very guilty. I drove him to a love suicide."

"Huguette, I'm in no position to talk about this. Dr. ___ is calling you at three this afternoon. She will address your concerns. Until then, please realize that Mori was a very troubled man, with plenty of reasons of his own to take his life. He had a history of mental ill-ness, on antidepressants for years, business in the red, dysfunctional relationship at home, failed marriage back in Japan, even a bout with prostate cancer which may well have left him impotent. The man suffered. Nothing to do with you. Here's your coat."

"I feel like I murdered him."

"You poor woman. We'll get you sorted and these feelings will go away. You're very lucky they're not charging you with anything. Focus on that." I slide my arms into the sleeves of the coat he's holding up for me, like a gentleman. I wish more men had his man-ners. The world would be so much nicer.

"Thank you."

* * *

Darjeeling for when I'm just glad to be home in my snug, little flat, after the outside world has battered me. If I were home-home, I'd pop a *pâte chinois* [ecitor's note, which I hope is not intrusive: the English rustic delicacy, shepherd's pie] in the microwave. They don't have that here, but on the upside, there's no Coralie to body shame me and I do have a frozen *tarte tatin* begging to be baked. Not as good as fresh, of course, but I could've spent the night in police custody with a streetwalker fresh in from Wuhan coughing all over me, so it's time to be grateful for small pleasures.

Yes! There is a god. The evidence: an unopened, unexpired tub of *crème fraîche* way in the back of the top shelf. Yes! All's well that ends well. That's from Shakespeare, which it's hard to believe some kids are taught in French. They miss all the jokes.

I'd so much love to take a long walk, but the streets of Paris are not safe. I miss

Masahisa. He's lucky, though, to have missed all this. They say it will only get worse. Masses of us will suffer and die.

Before I have a chance to get sucked into negative thoughts, my phone starts rejoicing with a FaceTime ring. I hesitate. The phone never hesitates; it's so smart, after all. It keeps on noisily announcing Christian. After all this hullabaloo, I feel like some silence, but I should take it.

"Hi, Christian."

"Hi, Huggie. Are you alright?"

"In what sense?'

"All senses."

"Yes and no. You? How's your mom?"

"She's fine, fine. We're all worried sick about you."

"About me? Don't be. So far, no dry cough or fever. Can I say hello to her?"

"Mom just drove into Gaspé for groceries. Gonna stock up on toilet paper and all that."

"How's the weather?"

"Joke?"

"Joke."

"Huggie, I'm really worried about you."

"Why?"

"Sweetie, I got a call from the Paris police and then another one from the Canadian embassy, consular division."

"Oh, you did?"

"Oh, I did? Huggie, I'm your husband. Why didn't *you* call me? You left me to hear from a third party that you'd been assaulted, lost your job, lost your best friend, witnessed a suicide? How could you not tell me?"

"I didn't want to disturb your visit to your mom. She's so nervous all the time."

"Listen, I'm coming home right away. You shouldn't be alone. We'll get through this."

"I heard they're suspending Air Canada flights pretty soon. Maybe I should come to you. We could wait it all out in the country."

"You'd go nuts in the Gaspésie. There's nothing to do but stare at snow. You need Paris. I'll come back tomorrow."

"No, Christian, seriously. It's different here. Like dystopian fiction. I'll use my air-miles before they expire."

"Huggie, did you have an affair with that guy? The dead man?"

"God, no. Don't you trust me?"

"They said you said it was a Japanese love suicide. That... that hurts."

"Didn't they also tell you I was con-fused? The psychiatrist says I was delusional, having a post-traumatic psychotic episode. I saw a stranger die right in front of me!"

"But what were you doing there?"

"Can we talk about this in person? I'm still in treatment, you know, and I get confused between what Dr. ___ tells me happened and what I remember."

"Ok, Huggie. Let's research flights and talk again later. I love you."

"I love you, too, Kissie."

* * *

No one can turn back the clock. Time cools and turns bitter like old tea. I wish I had ever had the time to follow Masahisa home, see his apartment. I'd like to have stood in the dark, under a black umbrella, immersed in the music of the falling rain, outside his bedroom window. I know there was a night I missed-- it happened without me-- when he clicked on a rice paper shaded floor lamp, but forgot to close the curtains. Or maybe he didn't forget; he felt like embracing his proximity to the wet night-- it's Paris after all, he didn't travel thousands of kilometers to shut it out. He loved that lamp. Its light hot-stone-massages the eyes, like a fireplace, like a pair of citrine earrings in a sauna. He stared at something on the opposite wall, then wandered idly about the room, touching his fingertips to surfaces absently, not really feeling them. His mind was on something else. He was waiting, but not with impatience. His back to the window, like maybe he was conscious, after all, of the exposure, he untied and re-tied his blue and white cotton *yukata*. Its print was abstract, diamonds repeating. She came in, hair dripping from the shower, soaking the shoulders of her almost-identical robe. Hers was the same diamond print, only inverted blue on white instead of white on blue. They must have bought them at Shizuka from Shizuka herself, a day I wasn't there. Masahisa advanced toward her, weightless. Two jellyfish in a lit tank, their bodies transparent, they came together, floating, blurred, wet, the animal synchronized.

The social worker, Rachida Something is supposed to call me or something tomorrow. That's good. She can help me find a new job. I think I'd like to be one of those police interpreters, or a Consular Service interpreter. My English is more than good enough. I have the scores to prove it. There's probably a practical exam each one asks you to take, too. I'm very confident I'd pass with flying colours. My first request to Rachida will be to research that. Next, maybe I'll see about going back to school part time, a Masters in something. She can help me with that. I've never worked with a social worker before. It could be great, like a life coach. But the shrink? No, thank you. Dr. ___ is surely a delusional sex addict, like the lot of them. The oven's beeping. It's preheated and ready for my well deserved apple pie. I think I'd like to visit the United States sometime soon. It's hard to believe I've never been, but when money is tight, you have to prioritize, and I always was saving up for my strolls along the Seine, solitary or on the arm of a handsome man, it doesn't matter which. Both are dignified lifestyles. I don't believe that a girl needs to starve herself silly and rip off all her body hair to satisfy some man just to have a fulfilling life. No, you can be your own soul mate, your own best companion. I don't paint my toenails blood red for men. No, they're scared of our blood anyway. I do it for myself.

Other titles by Hillary Raphael

OUTCAST SAMURAI DANCER

I LOVE LORD BUDDHA

BACKPACKER

XIMENA